THROUGH THE WALLS

MADDISON SLADE

Contents

1. Chapter 1 — 1
2. Chapter 2 — 5
3. Chapter 3 — 15
4. Chapter 4 — 20
5. Chapter 5 — 24
6. Chapter 6 — 33
7. Chapter 7 — 41
8. Chapter 8 — 48
9. Chapter 9 — 56
10. Chapter 10 — 65
11. Chapter 11 — 75
12. Chapter 12 — 82
13. Chapter 13 — 90
14. Chapter 14 — 99
15. Chapter 15 — 108
16. Chapter 16 — 117

17.	Chapter 17	127
18.	Chapter 18	137
19.	Chapter 19	147
20.	Chapter 20	158
21.	Chapter 21	168
22.	Chapter 22	178
23.	Chapter 23	188
24.	Chapter 24	198
25.	Chapter 25	208
26.	Epilogue	217

Chapter 1

"Reese!" A voice shouted, initially sounding far but then growing louder. "Get up, you have school," I say as I gradually open my eyes.

Poor idea!

It burns. I say, putting my midnight blue blanket over my head.I was only wearing a grey tank top and dark purple and black pyjama pants when my mother yelled, "C'mon," and she yanked the blanket totally off of me.

I moan and get into position before kicking my feet over the edge of the bed and sauntering towards the bathroom. I enter and close the door after me. I then splashed water on my face in an effort to wake up. I just carry on with the rest of my morning school routine after that. I wash my face, brush my teeth, put on some minimal makeup, get dressed, etc.

Generally speaking, I only like mascara and a minimal amount of eye shadow. I just apply a small amount of Chapstick if my lips are dry. My step-dad is still asleep, so I down the stairs quietly since I know what will happen if I wake him up.

Okay, I'm going now. I say quietly and give my mother a cheek kiss.

"Okay, I love you, see you tonight." She said after I had exited the door and was moving along the pavement.I waved as I walked towards the school. From my house, it would just take 5 to 10 minutes to walk there.

I went to my locker after I arrived at school. Adrienne, my best friend, was waiting for me there. I slow down as soon as I spot her and give her a wary look. She was nervously scanning the area while fiddling with the ring on her finger.

I say, "Hey," clearly jolting her out of her reverie.

She mumbles, "Hey," in response.

You all right? I quietly asked her.

"No," she answered. I had some concerns. She isn't typically like way. She has greater vivacity. She almost shrieked in my ear a split second later. "I'm hungry!" you say.

I laughed and said, "Okay, I think I have a candy bar in here." I said rummaging through my luggage. Just in case, I always have food in my bag. I at last located it! I grinned as I turned to face my closest friend. "Would you like the candy bar?"

She almost screamed at me, "Yes!"

I gave her a candy bar that I had taken out of my pocket. She grinned and bolted off laughing. I don't believe I ought to have given her that. By the time the day is over, she will unquestionably be high on sugar. Only one pub, there!

I placed my bag inside of my locker, picked up my books, and went to class. History was my first subject. This class has no pals for me.

My short brown hair is twirled in my fingers as I calmly listen to Mr Wong after entering the room from the back door and occasionally brush my swoopy fringe out of my blue eyes.

The class ended quickly, so I simply walked to my next class. This one was with Cameron, my other best friend. I entered to find a throng of people. My school has a lot of fights, so I know this is one of them. Just who it is, I'm not sure. I saunter over to the group of folks holding their phones. I gasp as I take in what is unfolding in front of me.

I see Cameron on the ground with a bleeding nose being repeatedly struck in the face by another powerful figure who is standing on top of him. I move in and push the boy away after removing him from Cameron. He simply gives me a confused and enraged stare. Probably curious as to who I am. Cameron was holding his nose as he stared at me in disbelief as I gazed down at him.

He continued to grab his nose to prevent blood from dripping onto the ground as he stood up. "What did you do now?" I moaned. The unidentified boy chuckled, "Me?! Why do you think I acted inappropriately? Cameron shouted.

You were on the floor getting punched in the face by him when I started, "Well," I said. What was it, given that you constantly do something? I asked, pointing to the young man who had dark brown hair that was almost black and bright blue eyes and appeared to be our age.

He added casually, "I made a comment on his player ways. Like you have room to discuss. Come on in and I'll tidy you up. I muttered the first sentence, but it was loud enough for him to hear.

The guy exclaims in a humorous manner, "Oh your girlfriend comes to save the day!"

I muttered, "I'm not his girlfriend.

She isn't even interested in you. While gazing at Cameron, he laughed.

Oh, stop talking. I remarked cleaning Cameron up and dragging him to the toilet. then going back to class.

There is just one seat left when we get there, and guess who it's beside. I laid my books down before settling into the chair behind the desk and slouching.

The boy said, "Hey."

I said, "Hey, mystery boy," without even looking at him.

He said out loud, "You were extremely disrespectful previously.

Indeed, and? I requested the start to scribble in my notepad.

Never imagined a gorgeous person like you could be so fierce. My cheeks slightly tinted as he stated this. Only because that had never been spoken to me before did I blush. I just can't get used to it.

Never previously have I heard that one. I respond rudely and eventually turn to face him.

He muttered something like, "Whatever gothic bitch."

My head was lowered as I gazed at my desk. All right, the flirtation ends here. He'll begin to tease me like the other students in the school. I'm picked on by freshmen, even though I'm a junior.

I moved towards the school's exit as I got ready to leave for home. I inhaled deeply and went outside knowing just what would happen when I came home.

CHAPTER 2

I simply listen while I stand at the end of the driveway. While contemplating whether or not to enter my house, I stand and listen.

I take a quick look at the neighbor's home. She was an elderly woman who frequently wore long gowns and had short, curling white and grey hair. Her husband had died a few years prior, she had no pets, her children were spread out across the country, and she lived alone.

As she emptied her trunk of groceries, she stumbled over them. I decided it would be best to assist her, and I did so. I'll assist, I'm here. I offered to pull out of the trunk of her red Subaru a plastic bag stuffed with paper towels and toilet paper.

She reacted a little startled and replied, "Oh, thank you sweetie."

I laughed out loud. I'm sorry; it was not my intention to terrify you.

"Oh no, it's okay, I'm still here, aren't I?" She questioned, but it was more of a declaration. She didn't have to carry them because I grabbed a bigger grocery bag and a bag full with cans.

I yelled "Okay" before closing the trunk and grabbing the final bag. "How are things going, Ms. Gretta?" As we stroll along the sidewalk, I made an effort to strike up a conversation by asking.

She gave a rather tepid, "I'm still kicking," in response. A. "And you?" She went on.

I echoed her tone, "Peachy," and said it.

She unlocked the door when we got there. I know I heard them. Despite being next door, I constantly hear them. How loud they must be when you're in the same house, I have no idea. As we reached the living room, she added while casting me a knowing glance. They were audible a few minutes ago. Was that the reason you were outdoors, standing there? Despite already knowing the answer, she inquired.

I avoided making eye contact and merely remarked, "Yeah, they've been fighting a lot more than usual lately." These discussions irritated me. They were strange and odd, and I was constantly afraid of offending them.

Why do you think that is, exactly? You can put them there, she said, indicating a tiny table in her kitchen, after asking. Her home was modest and unadorned, but it was still lovely.

"I don't know, I think the baby is probably to blame. hormones in general. I said as I placed the bags on the table.

She simply gave me a blank look. The question "What baby?" Oh, you're right, nobody is aware of that yet.

Mom made the decision to wait to notify anyone until we were all present. Adrienne and Cameron were completely unaware, and I wasn't even allowed to inform the neighbour woman.

Oh my, my mother is expecting. Do not tell anyone, please! Nobody should be aware, right? I begged, stating the first quickly.

I won't, so don't worry. She laughed as she made her vow, reassuring me.

I said, "Thank you," with relief. I grinned and said, "I'd better get home before she starts to worry." It's been twenty minutes since I typically entered the room.

She yelled out as I approached the door, "Okay, see you around, thanks for the help."

When I stepped up onto the porch leading to my house, there was silence, so I assumed they had stopped fighting and went inside. My step-dad was holding a bud light while lounging in the recliner. He was seeing television. I could tell he was inebriated, but when wasn't he?

Anything he could get his hands on, he would drink or smoke. It was repulsive. He was revolting, but I had to put up with him because he was my mom's husband. Since I was around five or six, I've lived here. Thirteen years of torture are involved.

I crept up the stairs in silence, thinking he wouldn't hear me, but they started to creak on the first one! I'm in trouble.The question, "Where were you?" He severely enquired. His eyelids were still closed when I gave him a quick glance. I made a U-turn and turned to gaze back at the top of the stairs. So near!

I was assisting the neighbour in bringing some items inside. I said slowly as I turned to face him, who was now resting against the living room door frame and gazing at me.

I'm shocked at how composed he's acting when he says, "Well, you should have told us where you were." He would typically be screaming and raving nonstop, if not more.

Mommy isn't here. I questioned, entirely dodging his inquiry. Why did I do that, I wonder? I'm positive I passed out or something.

He now appeared to be a little irate. He clinched his teeth and murmured, "She got tired and went to bed. Don't disturb her." At first, he was hesitant.

I said gently, looking aside, "Okay, I'll be quiet when I go to my room then." I then took a gentle step up the creaky stairs. I quickly lied, "I have homework," and he simply nodded as I was being observed.

After reaching the top, I turned to enter my room, but instead I hid behind a wall and waited until I heard him return to the couch. Just across the hall from mine was my mother's room, which I entered covertly. The only thing separating our rooms was a wardrobe. In the loo, I overheard crying. I quickly approached the door and attempted to open it, but it was locked. I softly knocked. She scrambled, and the door slid a little, so I assume she was pressed up against it.

When the door's latch turned, it slowly opened to show my mom, who had tear-soaked cheeks and raccoon eyes streaked with mascara."Reese!" She sounded startled and gasped. "Are you alright?" She cried out.

I grabbed her arm, dragged her to the bed and then sat her down, telling her, "Yes mum, I'm fine, but obviously you aren't."

She said, "I'm fine," but I didn't believe her. She was not okay! What did he do to her this time, I wonder.

"Why don't you just leave him?" I questioned in awe.

"I know it's hard to believe, but I'm pregnant and I love him and he loves me." She kept babbling. You see, that was my mother for you; she didn't give up easily, she had a strong personality, and she tried to find humour in even the most grave circumstances. Nevertheless, my mother was an extraordinary person. She was my naive heroine.

"Dad's weekend; are you sure you're going to be alright without me?" I rubbed her back while I questioned.

My father moved out when I was a young child, but he subsequently returned and fought for custody after my mum and dad divorced a while back. He simply received visitation rights; he was not given it. Every other weekend, I see him. He treats me well, but occasionally he doesn't show up.

She responded in a duh tone, "I'm a grown woman, I can take care of myself. I laughed at her because I was expecting it.

"Okay," I replied as I embraced her. She gave me a long hug in return, as if she didn't want to let go of me.

She ushered me out the door and added, "I'm going to bed now." That, however, suddenly altered.

She closed the door in my face, and I grinned. I yelled, "Good night," a little too loudly, and then laughed. I considered going to my dad's because he didn't pay much attention to me and was frequently out working when I was there. We conversed, but the topics that came up most often were financial difficulties or his attempts to engage me in conversation about my week. The most of my time with him during the holidays was spent with my aunt Penelope because he was at work.

I smiled as I remembered my aunt, who was the greatest someone could hope for. But because she hasn't been there as frequently, it's been a while since I've seen her. I nearly knocked myself off the door of my mother's bedroom when I turned around.

I told you to leave her alone, didn't I? That was not a query. He was indignant.

I just asked her if she planned to visit my father this weekend. I spoke quietly. I despised sounding frail and mushy. I detested how he treated me in this way. My life was awful.

I should have known you wouldn't listen when I warned you to leave her alone, though. He spoke quietly yet slightly yelling.

I snuck by him and went to my room. What did you anticipate? I'm an inquisitive teen. I responded lightheartedly, but it didn't take him long to start pursuing me. I continued, "I should complete my schoolwork right now.

He tightly gripped my arm as I was ready to walk up to my bedroom's door and yanked me onto one of the top stairs. He started to follow me as I backed down the steps gradually. Despite a few stumbles, I am able to stop myself before falling. Why do you have to meddle in what happens between me and your mother all the time? Mind your own business, please. Now that he was screaming, for some reason I decided to respond, which wasn't the wisest move. You would think that after having this happen so frequently that I would have learned my lesson by now, but I haven't.

I yelled, giving him a stern look, "It's my business when her life is at stake. Yes, that is all. Talk back to the inebriated, irate person. That is very clever. We were on the stairs but at the bottom of them. I informed him, "You know Ms. Gretta hears it.

He pushed me into the railing after grabbing hold of my shoulders. I was merely uneasy; he wasn't hurting me. "Well, nobody's said anything yet, so why do you think they'll say anything at all?" He questioned while grinning viciously. Additionally, unless you want your mother to be missing a daughter, neither your mother nor you will say anything, he threatened.

I initially kept quiet before acting foolishly as usual. "Have I already told anyone? No, I haven't, but don't think otherwise—I'm not afraid of you. You're just a violent alcoholic with temper problems, and I'll fight back one day. It wasn't my most smart line, but I delivered it with assurance and it was enough to make him lose his cool. When he pushed me, I had sharp back pains. My top was bent over as he continued to force me against the bannister, and I winced as he leaned in to shove me back even further.

"You're weak; neither you nor your mother will put up a fight."
He was accurate. I wouldn't speak, but you would respond in kind.
I wasn't emotionally fragile. I wasn't the strongest person there
physically, but I was more powerful than I appeared to be. The fact
that he forced me to construct barriers is one thing I can thank
him for. After a while, the pain of his blows became tolerable, even
though they were still painful.

I tried to lean up, but I was unable to do so because of a severe
backache. I wanted to cry, but I refused to give him that gratifi-
cation. I couldn't help but let a small gasp out of my mouth when
he pressed again. He really grinned in spite of the anguish he was
causing me. He has no compassion at all!

He released me, tossed me down the remaining stairs, and then
kicked me in the stomach. After saying that, he trudged back to the
living room and sank into his favourite recliner as if nothing had
occurred. There will likely be a bruise there tomorrow because it
hurts so much. My back is the most painful.

I got to my feet and headed to my bedroom. I had no homework
at all. I so simply sat there and thought about everything.

My book bag was slung over my shoulder. Since it was Friday,
my father will pick me up today about 6 o'clock. Adrienne was
standing there when I turned around after locking my locker.

"I didn't see you all day," she complained with a pout.

Oh, I'm sorry. On the way here, it started to rain, and as I didn't
have an umbrella, I took cover under a piece of furniture until the
rain subsided a little. She nodded while slightly scrunching her
face as I continued.

"That's why your hair is wet," she remarked, chuckling as she said
it.

I merely growled at her to "shut up."

We strolled cheerfully to the door when she clasped our arms together. My mother sees my best friend as a daughter, but I treat her like a sister. "Hey, did you hear about the new kids yet?" She inquired at random.

"Nope, what are their names?" I responded by requesting.

She started to continue, but a recognisable voice interrupted her. "Well the girls name is Brianna and the guys name is-"

Cameron was brutally beat by "Graham," a mysterious boy. He had a good look about him.

When I looked at Adrienne, she was completely perplexed. Her jaw was almost touching the ground. Graham said, "I hear he's really hot."

I muttered something repetitive and rolled my eyes, "Sounds like someone's got a crush."

Maybe I do," he replied with a grin. I understood his meaning.

, "I knew you were gay!" I responded and started to make my way back to the door, dragging Adrienne after me this time.

"I'm straight!" you declare. His scream was audible across the entire hallway.

I responded, "Yeah, about as straight as a circle." I have nothing at all against folks who preferred the same sex. Actually, at my old school, I had some incredible friends who shared the same sexual preferences. To me, they were the most dependable and trustworthy people I've ever known. They never judged me because they knew what it was like to be teased. Though it had been a while since I had seen them, I missed my old buddies. I might attempt to contact Mike at some point. He gave me the largest hug ever when I left a few years ago, I still remember that. I believed I was going to pass away.

Graham took hold of me and pushed me up against a tiled wall in the hallway. Thankfully, it was only the two of us; otherwise, word would have spread like wildfire. This was only our second meeting. I felt discomfort in my back almost immediately. I anticipated there would be a bump. As the anguish persisted, all I could do was squint my eyes.

Want me to demonstrate it? I gasped, arched my back, and dug my chest into his, but he didn't seem to care; instead, he just got a really bewildered look on his face and backed away, asking, "I'm sorry, are you okay? He pushed on me a bit harder, but that was enough to for me to gasp and arch my back. I apologise for hurting you.

"It's not your fault I just-" uh-oh, oh, "fell," I said. Really fluid, Reese.

Oh, okay. May I check on you to see if everything is okay? He enquired as he drew nearer.

"Oh no, I'm fine, just a little sore, that's all." I felt awful about lying. He appeared to be a decent man. Besides the fact that he assaulted Cameron. I said, "I have to go home before my mother gets furious.

He responded, still perplexed, "Oh okay umm see you Monday," as Adrienne and I sprinted for the door.

"What actually occurred?" Once we were out of earshot of him, she questioned.

"I fell, that's really what ha-" I was terminated. I was confident that she would expose my lies. Since we were little, we have known one another. I was raised here. I merely attended a different school. My mother got tired of driving me an hour and a half to two hours away every day, so I had to switch schools. In addition, Jay, my stepfather, complained. Despite the fact that this school's education isn't as good as my prior ones, I still like it.

"No, you lied to him, but he doesn't know you well enough to know that, and I'm going to spill," I said. With her arms crossed, she demanded.

Will you have a look at it? Sighing, I enquired.

She gave me a long look before realising that I was unwilling to discuss anything at the time. She said, "Turn around."

She lifted up my grey shirt after I complied with her instructions and gasped. uh-oh!"Oh, my God!" It's extremely horrible, Reese, she exclaimed. She said, sounding worried, "I think you should go to the hospital.

"No, it's okay. It doesn't hurt unless you touch it, and it'll go away in a couple of days." She merely gave me a look as I pulled my shirt back down and made up an excuse.

She angrily replied, "I want an explanation when you get back from your dad's, and if it's not gone, you're going to the hospital." Knowing I wouldn't succeed in this, I nodded to her. I walked home after that and got ready to visit my dad.

CHAPTER 3

I sat on the porch with my arms tightly crossed on my chest, It was spring but it was still a little chilly out. It was nine and my mom had left for work around eight but when she left she gave me a pitiful look as if to say 'I'm sorry'. Yeah my dad was late but I was used to it he always came eventually, at least he cared that much.

The tv was blaring from inside the house and I was sure we were bound to get a noise complaint. Once my mom left, my step dad threw me out the door along with my bags and told me to wait outside for my real dad because I was making him mad. He had the volume turned up so loud I'm surprised the state of Alaska didn't complain and we were in Ohio! The sounds of guns going off and yelling filled the streets, I had no clue what he was watching probably something about war.

After about twenty minutes a black Cadillac pulled up outside the house. The window rolled down and it was my dad. He climbed out, grabbed my bags and put them in the trunk as I slid in the passengers seat. "New car?" I asked in attempt to make conversation. These talks were always awkward.

"Yeah do you like it?" He asked.

"Yeah it's comfortable as well as classy," I responded.

"Look I'm sorry about being late I honestly just lost track of time" he said looking a little guilty.

His blue eyes filled with guilt, I couldn't help but cave. "It's okay I understand," I said with a smile. I couldn't help but notice all the guilt fall out of his eyes as soon as the words escaped my mouth.

"I have a surprise for you when we get back to my apartment," he said excitedly.

"What is it? Can I have a hint?" I bombarded him with a ton of questions until we finally reached the apartment complex in Cleveland.

I opened the door but nothing was there I turned around with a confused look on my face and he followed me in the door. I then shut it and behind the door was my surprise."Aunt P!" I shrieked.

"Hey," she said back with a smile on her gorgeous face. She looked a little different from the last time I saw her, now she had dark brown hair with an inverted bob style.

"It been so long!" I exasperated wrapping my arms around her neck. She was about my height and I was short.

She chuckled hugging me back tightly. I looked over and my dad was standing in the kitchen watching us through the pass-through with a small smile gracing his lips.

"How'd you get in here? You don't have a key and there was no one in here to let you in." He asked giving his sister a knowing look.

"I have my ways," she did with a smirk before turning to me. "You better get some sleep, we're going shopping tomorrow!" She yelled excitedly.

****

I slept for what seemed like a couple hours before a hand shook me awake."Morning," the soft voice said.

"Morning," I mumbled back. "What time is it?" I asked rubbing my tired eyes and looking at my blurry aunt who was slowly becoming clear.

"Uhh maybe five or five thirty," she trailed off. It was then that I realized it was still dark outside, well as dark as Cleveland gets.

I looked at her in disbelief and moved my head in small circles while scrunching up my face. She began laughing at me and motioned me to the restroom.

I took a shower, dried my hair, got dressed, and did my makeup lightly within an hour. I was wearing my black, ripped jeans and my white and black jersey shirt with the number 19 on the front in red, then I paired the outfit with my black and white converse. Which just so happened to be the only pair I brought.

After both my aunt and I were ready we quietly slipped out the door of the apartment leaving my snoring dad asleep on the couch.

We drove for a good amount of time but it only felt like an hour or so because we were jamming out to the radio. Rock, pop, etc...

"Oh, well imagine, as I'm pacing the pews in a church corridor and I can't help but to hear, no I can't help but to here an exchanging of words." The lyrics blasted through the speakers as we sang along and I drummed my fingers on the dash-board.

We parked in a parking lot outside of a store and slipped in the doors. After a couple hours my feet began to hurt and we weren't even close to being done. She dragged me into Victoria's Secret and we bought a couple bras and two hoodies. Mine was black and hers was white but they had the same design.

I missed having my aunt around she was one of the only people I trust and she treated me like I was equal, not a punching bag or anything of the such. My mom was the same way and they still hung out sometimes even though my mom and dad weren't together.

I sighed dropping the bags at my feet and then breathing a laugh as my aunt turned on the ignition and sat back. "Did you have fun?" She asked grabbing my attention.

"Is that a serious question?" I questioned but continued before she could answer, "of course I did, I always have fun with you."

"Great!" She exclaimed. "And now we go home and find your dad, woo." She said in a unenthusiastic tone but I just smiled knowing she was kidding and that she loved her brother.

"Dad wake up," I put my hand on his shoulder in attempt to wake him from his slumber.

"John if you don't get up I will do unmentionable things," my aunt mused from behind me. My dad opened his eyes and looked up at me with an emotionless expression that was soon replaced by annoyance.

"I need to finish this paper and then I'm done," he said but I could smell the alcohol that's laced his breath as he spoke.

"John I'm taking Reese home in the morning so you don't have to bother." My aunt snapped in a harsh tone. "You can see her the next time she comes up," she continued, a scowl evident on her face.

"I didn't want her to come down this time! You made me pick her up and bring her here, you have been since she was ten! Even if it was through a phone call! I didn't want her here and I don't want her here now!" My father shouted at the top of his lungs.

My heart stopped in my chest. This is my real dad. The one who should love me. He doesn't though, and I should have known.

"Come on Reese lets get you home now." My aunt suggested with sad eyes obviously not seeing the point in arguing with my dad.

When we arrived at my house the doors were locked and the lights out. "Can you get in?" My aunt asked.

"Yeah I have a key," I lied.

"I'm sorry about your dad, I'm sure he didn't mean any of that." She tried to comfort me but it wasn't working.

"Oh really because he seemed pretty sure of himself." I laughed humorlessly and looking at her as my dad did me, absolutely emotionless.

I got my bags out of the truck and my aunt drove off as I walked to the porch and sat on the steps waiting for morning so my mom would let me in. I sigh as I a hand through my hair. "This is going to be a long night," I murmur to myself.

CHAPTER 4

I t was an abnormally cold night for spring. It felt like it was in the twenties but who knows.

I can't feel my feet. I thought as I moved my bag onto the step above me and used it as a pillow.

I can't help but think over the things my dad had said to me. His words were taunting me. I decide that laying on my porch steps was cold and uncomfortable. So I call my best friend Adrienne.

Ring. Ring. After the third ring I realized that it was four in the morning and it's wrong to call her at this hour. Plus, she's probably asleep and I shouldn't wake her up, but just as I went to hang up. "Hello?" She muttered groggily.

"Uhhh sorry, did I wake you?" I asked. That's stupid of course you woke we up, dipshit.

"Yeah, but it's fine what's up?" She was genuinely interested and her voice held slight concern.

"My dad brought me home early and my mom locked her door so I can't get in. I was wondering if you could come get me.If not that's okay I can wait or call Cameron," I rushed the last part.

"Nah it's cool I'm on my way." She said and I heard shuffling on the other end of the call.

"Thanks," I said monotonous. I felt bad for making her do this.

Within the next hour I was at her house and we were sprawled across her red colored bed shoving popcorn in our mouths as we watched Ghost Whisperer. Soon the episode was off and another was about to begin but, of course, there were commercials.

"So what happened to your back?" She asked getting straight to the point. I think her curiosity was eating her alive all this time because she was looking at me expectantly waiting very impatiently for an answer.

I had to come up with a good excuse quick because otherwise she would see right through me. My mind went hopelessly blank. "Promise you won't tell anyone," I said stalling, but then I thought of an accurate excuse.

"Promise," she said.

"Because it's really embarrassing," I said holding off my lie just to annoy her.

"Oh just tell me already I'm going insane!" She nearly screamed in my face.

I took a breath and began. "I was on the stairs, just kinda standing around and I lost balance and fell over the railing backwards." I said cracking up a little at just how accurate that could be. I would do that but unfortunately that wasn't the case.

She looked at me with a blank face before bursting out into fits of laughter but once she calmed down and just giggled she managed to stamper out, "h-how c-can you lose your balance standing?"

"I don't know but I did it," I said laughing a little.

"Is it looking any better?" She questioned getting a little serious.

Should I lie? Or should I tell her the truth? Maybe I'll tell her everything... No, I can't, no good would come of that. "A little better but not much," I say shrugging my shoulders.

"Maybe you should get it checked out," she suggested.

"Nah I'll be fine it's just a bruise," I brushed it off quickly.

"Yeah, one that takes up your entire lower back. It's totally nothing to worry about." She mumbled under her breath just loud enough for me to hear, the last part laced in sarcasm. I waved my hand dismissively at her and she rolled her eyes. I had dropped the subject and she let it go.

The rest of the night was just us goofing off and laughing until we couldn't breathe. I loved my best friend, she could take your mind off anything and cheer you up fast. It was times like these that I needed her but I would never admit that. She was helping me and she didn't even know it.

In the morning we ate breakfast and hung out until about 9am, then I went home and immediately went to my room. Jay leaves around six in the morning on week days for work. On weekends he watches tv all day then around nine he goes to the local bar.

He would usually go to work, building houses and other con-structions. He is a General Laborer. After work he comes home to take a shower and freshen up after that it's about nine at night or so depending on what time the job got done, he would then head to the bar called The Iron Skillet, It had great food but it was still a bar and I was only seventeen so if my mom went she would bring me back some of their food, but normally Jay wouldn't come back until three or four in the morning. He was almost always drunk but on week days when he had to work he drank a little less.

He had anger problems and if I did something wrong he would hit me to teach me a lesson. For example, one time I didn't shut the door all the way so he punched me in the stomach. Although I deserved it, he hits me when I talk back. When my mother fights with him it's worse. I try to find some place else to stay when I can but I don't want to bother anyone so I keep to myself. Nobody knows but I desperately want to tell Cameron and Adrienne. Maybe they wouldn't tell. No of course they would. They would want to protect me. Right now my mom and I are on our own.

I got hungry, so I went down stairs quietly. I tip-toed across the living and dining rooms and into the hall. Then once I reached the kitchen I saw my mom standing in front of the fridge. I didn't think she was home. She turned and saw me and then opened the door of the freezer. "I was wondering where you were, I was just going to wait for you." She looked at me quizzically, she probably didn't know I was here either.

"Yeah I've been here for an hour," I replied.

"Well it's only four, are you hungry?" She asked me.

"Yeah, I was just coming down here for some food." I admitted and she smiled slightly.

"We'll go out to eat together," she offered with hidden excitement. "Just the two of us," she quickly added after seeing my reaction. I guess I made a face, thinking Jay would be there.

"Just the two of us," I reminded.

"Yes," she assured me.

"Then sure," I smiled.

"Great and I have some place I want to go, other than the restaurant of course." She giggled shutting the door to the freezer.

"Of course," I responded. "And where might that be?"

"We're going to take a trip down memory lane," she said cryptically walking out of the kitchen but I followed her.

"Tell me where we're going!" I exclaimed grabbing my leather jacket.

"It's a surprise!" She said with a smile on her face that was spread from ear to ear and we walked to the car.

CHAPTER 5

The car ride was short and before I knew it we were outside of the towns diner. It was small but we were a small town anyways.

As soon as I step inside the smell of pizza almost blew me back out the door. The aroma was very strong but it smelt delicious. I followed my mom to the last booth on the left side. Each booth had a picture of a landscape on the wall above our heads and red cushion seating. The booths line the walls on left and right. Through the middle, it had two tables and six chairs with the same red cushion at each one. It was very old country. There was a glass container under the cash register, towards the entrance that held deserts.

"What do you want to eat?" My mother questioned.

"Do you just want to order a medium pizza and share?" I suggested to her as she eyes the desert sections. Normally I wouldn't share my food as a matter of fact I hated it, but she was my mom and it would be less money. She could use the extra cash.

"Sounds fine to me." She said closing her menu.

After we eat, we head back to the car and mom drives in the opposite direction of our house. We pass lots of streets and buildings, but we're still in our little town of Dennison. Mom parks in a paved area then gets out and I do the same.

We walk into a park that looks vaguely familiar. There was a side walk that went all the way around the park. In the grass there was a little boy playing with a dog that looked like a pug and a woman sitting on bench near by. A man came and sat by her. The boy ran into the woman's arms, who I'm guessing is his mother, and the man, probably the father, wrapped his arms around both of them.

I really wish I could have a family like that, they are whole and they love each other. I have my mom though and that's all I need. She loves me even if my dad doesn't want me it's okay because other people have it ten times worse so I should be happy with what I have and not complain.

The back of the park is lined by trees. I noticed that, that's where my mom is heading to. She walks into the woods.

"Where are we going?" I asked nervously. I shouldn't be nervous. What's wrong with me?

"I'll show you, just follow me." She says then continues walking. I do as I'm told.

We pass more and more trees. Ducking under some branches so we don't get hit in the face. After about five minutes of walking through trees we reach the destination.

"This is it," she says moving a couple branches and gesturing for me to walk through. As I step out I immediately know the scene in front of me.

"The railroad tracks," I breathe out.

My mom had taken me here before many times. It was our safety place. It was always peaceful and quiet. The tracks must have been shut down or something because there were no trains on it ever. I loved this place, I missed this place. I haven't been here since I was thirteen and now I'm seventeen.

"I remember this place and I remember why we couldn't come back." I spoke but my mom gave me a worried look after noticing the darkness in my eyes.

"Well we're back now. I missed being here as well." She said walking over to the tracks. It was filled with rocks and beside the tracks there were cement blocks that we put there. I don't know why we did but to me, it was my way of claiming the tracks. We must have walked those tracks over five thousand times.

"Yeah, until he finds out," I sneered. Remembering the event. He had came and beat both of us. Ripping me away from my mom and telling us how despicable we were. He had locked me in a room, not letting me leave, for a week.

"He won't take it away from us again I promise." She noted seriously. It sounded like she was trying to convince herself.

"Okay," I said as we walked the tracks. "Why do you stay with him?" I've asked this more times than I can count.

"We love each oth-," that's as far as she got before I interrupted.

"He treats you like shit." I said monotonous.

"Reese Maire, language!" My mother scolded. My middle name was the same as my moms. Her full name was Madelyn Marie Laden. Laden was my step dad's last name, so I was the only Fode in the house and I felt very out of place, but I always did.

"I'm only stating the truth." I said as I kicked some rocks while I walked.

She sighed, "It's true we love each other, and I know you think he's a bad guy but he's just like every other one." She started to lie again.

"No he's not, other guys aren't like that," I exasperated.

"Yes they are, we are in love because that's what love is," she defended both herself and Jay. She was angry with me. I knew it, but I was just as angry with her.

"Love is nothing like that, he should care if you get hurt not be the one to hurt you!" I shouted at her. I'm being disrespectful and I know it but she's wrong.

She tried to ignore what I said because she knows it's true. "That's what love is, that's how life is and the sooner you realize that the better." She yelled, her eyes widening as she did so.

"Oh okay, so it's normal to cry almost every night and fight just about everyday." I stop to face her, giving her a skeptical look.

She opens her mouth to talk but shuts it again so I continue, "I can hear your sobs and when you fight, I can hear you yelling, then when he hits you I hear your screams and it terrifies me." Her eyes become glassy as I press the tips of my fingertips into my chest gesturing to myself. "But that's life right." I shrug at her.

"I'm sorry I-" she started again but it seemed that interrupting her was my speciality tonight. Normally if it was me I would blow up because I loathe being interrupted.

"I'm not the only one that hears it, the neighbor confronted me about it." I said shaking my head.

"We lov-" and yet again I'm stopping her. I'm just so tired of her excuses. She loves him and he can't love because he's heartless. I want to know the truth.

"But you don't care because you 'love' each other and it's completely normal for a married couple to be the same way you guys are, right? Then I suppose it's normal for me to be scared all the time and I can't let my guard down or make any friends because I'm too afraid they'll get hurt. He hits me and cuts me and he hurts me all the time and I know it's not normal and I know you won't protect me because your too afraid to. So I have to protect everyone else, I have to. I have to protect Cameron and Adrienne because I couldn't live with myself if they got hurt. I know there's another reason you won't leave him and I'm done with the lies.

Tell me the truth, now!" I'm almost in tears now. She just drops her head and starts to speak.

She clears her throat. "We do love each other," she said weakly and I scoff. "Let me finish," she demands. "We are having a baby and I want this child to have a father and I want to give her the best life possible, one that I failed to give you." She trailed off. "I want to make up for it and I want to make everyone happy, I'll do anything to make everyone happy."

"He can't make anyone happy." I say darkly.

"That's not true, he makes me happy."

"By hitting you."

"He's not always like that, he's caring and loving and he's different. I promise," she says. I've known him for a really long time now and he's never been like that, not when I was there at least, but she married him for a reason and they're having a kid, so maybe he is different... No he's still an ass and my moms still stupid, but I feel for her so I'll just let her do her own thing. I can keep mostly to myself and just avoid him. I have to stay anyways, I have to protect the baby.

I hug her and she cries. "Okay I'll give him a chance but if he messes it up I'm fighting back."

"He just has a different way of handling himself. I give you permission to fight back," she says nodding but we're still hugging. I didn't need her permission.

Then I let her go to face her, "I was gunna do it anyways."

She laughs a bit. Then we walk and talk for a while. We laughed and had a decent time. We went home and she told me we should go back there more often and I agreed. Then she said she missed me and hugged me. I hesitated for a moment. I didn't really like being hugged or touched. I felt uncomfortable and I wasn't used to it. I just really didn't like it, but I reluctantly returned the hug and smiled weakly. Then I went straight to my room.

The next day at school when I walked into my first period class I saw someone who wasn't usually there, and a girl that I didn't recognize. I sat down in my seat and the teacher entered. I slumped into my seat crossing my feet and putting my hands in my grey hoodie pocket.

The teacher mumbles something to the girl and boy and then pulls them to the front of the class. "Class this is Graham Winters," he says pointing to Graham. "and this is Brianna Winters his sister." He points to the girl with dark brown hair and green eyes. She's short and slender and her make up is perfect. She even dresses a little like me.

"You can take your seats at the back beside Mrs. Fode. I'm sorry that your so far back normally we would have the new students sit at the front but there's not a lot of seats up here and besides I don't think it'll be a problem with your grades." Mr. Ford said walking back to his desk smiling at the pair. We always make comments on his name. Normally the athletes would crack jokes involving cars.

They both took seats on either sides of me. The girl turned to me. "I'm Brianna but I'm sure you already know that." She introduced herself laughing a little.

I nod with a slight smile, "I'm Reese."

"That's such a unique and beautiful name," she complimented.

"Thanks," I say pressing my lips together.

"Okay... what kind of music do you listen to?" She asks.

I love music it's how I pass my time normally. So I decide to contribute a little to the conversation. "Three Days Grace, Panic at the Disco, Seether, Shinedown, etc." I said looking at her.

"Really me too," she said but then continued. "What's your favorite song by Three Days Grace?"

"Either, Never Too Late or Animal I Have Become."

"Same," she says. I think I could really like this girl.

She smiles brightly and then the teacher calls our attention. "Can I sit with you at lunch this is my first day and I don't have any friends," she laughs awkwardly in embarrassment.

"Sure I'll introduce you to mine," I say then turn to the teacher.

"Thanks," she whispers and I nodIn acknowledgment.

I start to feel like I'm being watched and I become uncomfortable and start to fidget in my seat. I look to my left and my blue eyes make direct contact with bright blue ones of the same color, that bore into me. We don't break the eye contact. I soon realize the familiar blue eyes belong to Graham. He smirks then began to speak. "Guess what Reese," he says.

"How do you know my name?" I ask curiously.

"I asked around," he shrugged. Yeah, because that's not creepy. "Anyways, guess."

"Uhh, your changing schools?" I asked crossing my fingers.

He glares at me. "No, I'm in all your classes now," he claps. "Along with my sister," he gestures towards her.

I blink, then again and again.... WHAT, no he's not.

He smirks again then adds, "and you're supposed to show us around and to all our classes."

Oh, boy. I take a deep breath. "Okay, I'll show you around."

I checked with the secretary and he was right, unfortunately. It had been a week since then but Brianna adapted to our group quickly and easily. Everyone liked her, Adrienne and Cameron and I. She was a cool person and she fit in perfectly. The popular people were beginning to get mad that she hung out with us. I guess they wanted another person to humiliate and ruin, then turn into one of them. I'm not letting that happen though, she didn't deserve that. I can save her from becoming a Barbie doll.

I trudged into my science class and sat in my seat. I was late, as usual. The teacher just ignored me and began her lesson. "We're doing group projects for the next month, but I'm choosing your partners so don't get to excited." Great I'm going to end up being with some loser who won't do the work or some nerd who will do it all and I don't have a problem with that one.

"Chole and Jonathan," name after name was called until there there were was only four people left but then..."Reese and Graham." Ugh why?

"Looks like we're partners now, huh." He whispered in my ear. Ew

"Yeah so you better help," I say.

"These partners are permanent," the teacher chimes. oh no.

"Don't worry I will, I could also help with other things." Graham smirked. this is going to be a long month.

"Shut up," I say glaring at him and he just laughs.

The teacher begins to announce the first project. "Okay first you will be building a volcano out of clay and such, but it has to actually erupt so I'm going to give you your types of volcanos now before the bell rings and you'll have to work on them in class and at home."

"Hear that we get to hang out," Graham pokes my side and I jump. He smirks and tries again but I grab his finger and bend it back, "ouch." He breathes then laughs when I let him go. "Feisty," he teases.

We got a fisher volcano. After being teased all day and hanging out with my friends for a while I head home. Then up to my room being as quiet as possible when my phone starts to ring very loudly. I struggle to shut it off and once I do I listen for a moment. I go to take a breath of relief but it gets stuck in my throat when I hear a door slam shut and stomping from up stairs.

I run to the bottom of the stairs but that's as far as I got before I turn to see my fuming step dad with his right fist clenched and the other grips a beer bottle that's almost empty at the top of the stairs.

Well shit.

Chapter 6

I can see that Jay's knuckles are beginning to turn white while holding on to the neck of the beer bottle. My eyes widen a little in fear.

He scrunched his nose up. Then he picked his hand up and threw the glass bottle of Budweiser to the ground. The glass shatters and falls down the steps, a couple pieces reaching the step above me.

He walked down until he was in front of me. I couldn't move or breath. I just stood there watching him, like an idiot. He was towering over me with a scowl on his face. "You are loud," he growled at me.

"You weren't sleeping." I said with an emotionless expression.

"I was in the bathroom and I was just going back to the bedroom to sleep but now I'm wide awake, thanks to you." His voice becomes louder with each word.

"Well I'll try to be quiet from now on okay?" I said, a little snippy.

"Don't be smart with me!" Jay grabs my shoulders and slams me into the front door. My breathing is staggered as my back hits the door.

Currently, my back is still a little bruised but it's a lot better and it doesn't even hurt anymore. Maybe it'll be gone be next week.

"I'm not being smart. It's not my fault you're mentally challenged." I spat, "you know people can help you with that, you're not alone, it's okay." I continue feigning care.

His eyes narrow into slits and his nostrils flare with anger. Then, he lets me go with one last push to the door. I thought he was done, I thought I was safe, I thought wrong.

Just as I took a breath, which I must have been holding. He smirks, oh no. His fist, that were balled tightly, collided with my lower rib and I swear I heard something crack. Pain shoots up my front and my stomach swirls. I groan in agony and clutch my stomach as I buckle over to the floor. My eyes begin to tear from the pain but I will not cry, especially not in front of him. I slowly get to my feet staring daggers into him as I do so.

He looked a little shocked, his eyes no longer returning my glare. I'm having trouble breathing but I'm positive nothing's broken. I've had broken bones before and it felt a lot worse than this, so I'm fine. He takes a moment before grabbing a hand full of my hair and ripping my head back.

"Don't ever talk back to me again and don't even bother standing up for yourself, it'll get you in even more trouble." My step dad sneers. "You disgust me. Just clean this up!" He commands in a sharp tone, releasing my hair and stepping over the shards of glass as he walks up the stairs, rounds the corner, and enters his room. I sigh in return and begin to pick up the pieces of the broken bottle.

I go up stairs after hours of scanning the steps for anymore glass and just leaving the little spot of wet beer at the top of the steps, I'll clean that up later.

I can't just keep taking this. it's ridiculous!

I walk to my room and lie in my bed that's pushed up against the wall farthest from the door. My dark brown dresser at the foot of my bed has a picture of my mom, aunt, and me. I move over to the picture and hold it to my chest before moving back to my bed. I take my ear buds and play some Shinedown. If You Only Knew blasts into my ears. I can hear a faint sound over my music but I ignore it at first, it became more annoying but the second so I take out my ear buds with a forceful jerk.

"I told you I was at work!" My moms voice yells.

"No you weren't, you were probably messing around with some guy. You must think I'm stupid." My step dad's voice booms. They do this all the time, he accuses my mom of cheating and she denies it and they keep screaming until it stops and usually it stops because he hits her or he throws something or she does, it's just tiring.

"Yes I'm the one cheating, if you think I don't know that you've been with some women since we were together, then your wrong!" My mom shrieks. There're so loud!

I need a new room in this house or just a completely different place all together. Their yells and screams are louder than ever tonight. Which is only adding to my headache that I now have from my hair being practically ripped out of my head.

A loud crashing sounds from the room across the hall. I immediately shoot up and fling my door open out if instinct, I guess. I walk across the hall to the door of my mom and Jay's room. I hear a scream and open the door. There is a white plate broken on the floor and mom is on the bed holding her arm and my step dad was standing up to the side of her looking at me.

"Are you okay, mom?" I ask eyeing her arm. Small trickles of blood were seeping through the cracks between her fingers.

"Yeah I'm-" she began but never got to finish.

"Shes fine, what makes you think you can just walk in like that?" My step dad interrupts.

"Did I ask you?" I retorted to him.

"Does it matter?" He snapped back.

"Stop it you two!" My mom shouts. "Go to your room," she orders me. I slam the door shut and head to my room. That's the last straw.

I clean the house Tuesday night and it looks nice, I'm proud of my work. I walk into the dinning room and then into the kitchen to finish the dishes. While waking down the hall to go to the bathroom I get distracted. The basement door, I open it and turn on the light, I step down the wooden stairs and notice that it's not really used that much and there's a television down here. I smile brightly determination shining in my eyes as I begin to clean it.

I gather my books walking into my science class followed by Graham. We sat in our seats which happened to be right beside each other because we were partners. "Okay since you didn't show yesterday we need to get to work, this is one of the only classes I'm having trouble in along with math and literature. We need to meet outside of school and get caught up." Graham announces.

"Okay," I said simply.

"Okay, like tonight," he said I little shocked that I agreed so easily.

"Would you be willing to meet me at the diner?" I asked

"Sure thing," he said eyeing me suspiciously.

At lunch I sat with my usual group and it was a usual day, Adrienne and I joked around. I hit her shoulder she hit me back then within a matter of seconds we were wrestling like animals and Cameron and Brianna had to break us up but we came apart laughing like hyenas. It was all okay and normal, well as normal as we get, until Holly Cherish came over.

Holly Cherish is the schools most popular girl. She probably slept with every one of the football players in Dennison High School even the seniors but we're only juniors and is currently after the fresh meat or Graham Winters. She's got it out for me and I didn't even do anything to her, well not that I know of.

"Hey Brianna, how are you?" Holly chirps as our laugher dies down.

"Umm, I'm okay." She says as Holly and her followers sit down at our table.

"How would you like to go shopping with us? We're having a shopping spree and we're all getting dresses for the upcoming dance." Holly says, Brianna looks around our table as if asking if it was okay. When she looks to me I just shrug.

She turns back to Holly and smiles. "I guess so, that sounds fun, when?"

"Tonight, right after school."

"Okay see you then. I'll wait outside the doors."

"Cool, later." Holly waves her fingers and walks away. Swinging her hips in attempt to be sexy. Ew, I want to look away but I can't! It's just so disturbing.

I'm sat in a booth at the diner with my notebook and a pencil in the seat beside me. I'm just waiting on Graham. Later in the day he said he would be here at 4:30 and right now it's 4:25. I came here right after school to avoid going home, I've been sitting here since. A bell rings, which indicates a person entering the place. Not expecting it to be Graham, I kept my gaze on the table.

"Hey, why are you here so early?" I hear his voice and I look up.

"It's only three minutes early." I state, checking the clock.

"Well, I figured you'd be late. Actually I didn't think you'd show up at all." He admitted, sitting down.

"Well I'm here," I say.

"I can see that." He watches me before starting again. "After looking up what a fisher volcano was, I found out that it's not going to be very easy."

"You had to look up the definition?" I ask him incredulously.

"Yeah, you already knew what it was didn't you?" He asks sheepishly.

I nod and smile widely, "it's not going to be that hard."

"It's not even an actual volcano, it shouldn't count." Graham mutters slumping in his seat.

I laugh, "okay do you have any ideas?"

We set there and brain storm for an hour and we order some pizza. After we come up with what we're going to do and how we're going to do it, we make another date to meet up but this time it's not at a restaurant.

"You're mean," he pouts as a move my chocolate desert out if his reach.

"Well if you want some then go buy some." I say, gesturing to the door.

He huffs and continues walking muttering something about no money.

I chuckle and shake my head walking with him. "Yeah I'm the mean one."

"You are." he whines, childishly.

"The first day I met you, you were beating up my best friend." I say looking at him with tired eyes.

"Oh yeah," he says scratching the back of his head.

"Oh yeah," I repeat to him. "I'm not even supposed to talk to you because he gets mad. Not to mention I'm mad at you for that."

"Oops," he says smiling cutely and shrugging.

I roll my eyes and laugh beginning my walk home and telling him goodbye. Once I arrive there I step inside and head to my room. I've cleaned the basement up completely and piled all the junk in a part of the room so I can move it out easily. We've always used the basement as storage and we barley go down there. I go up stairs into my room and pack all my stuff in boxes then take them to the basement. Then take the junk up stairs to my room. I was going to move into the basement. It was all set up. I just have to unpack and touch it up a bit.

On my way back down the stairs to go to the basement. I hear a soft voice, "Reese?" I look up and my mom is standing in the stairs shaking badly with tears running down her face. I run to her and ask what's wrong.

"There's something wrong with the baby." Those words shock me like an electric chair.

"How do you know?" I ask grabbing my coat and fishing through my moms purse for her car keys.

"I went to the bathroom and I'm bleeding but I'm not on my period." She sounds so scared and fragile. I look up at her worried.

"Are you sure?" I ask after finding the keys.

"Yes," she breathes. With that I'm running to the car and turning it on. I run back and help her to the car.

We arrive at the hospital and they take her immediately. Soon after she comes out with a tear free face, which relives me a little. She's showing but not to much, and I just noticed this.

"False alarm, everything's okay," she says and we hug each other. Soon after that we're in the car but I'm in the passenger seat this time, she refused to let me drive. I'm seventeen, besides I'm not that bad of a driver.

"I'm sorry I was sure something was wrong." My mom says, glancing at me.

"It's okay," I say. "But if you ever scare me like that again you're in so much trouble." I joke, only it wasn't really a joke. I almost pissed myself.

She laughs and looks at me. "I was wondering what you're doing in the basement." She speaks curiously.

"I'm taking over the basement. I moved all the stuff up into my room and all my stuff down there." I say nonchalantly.

"Oh, that explains a lot. Well at least we can get to our junk easier and we're farther away from you." She mutters quietly to herself.

"Hey!" I shout in protest.

She begins to laugh and throws her head back."I'm just kidding."

"Mm okay," I say sarcastically.

"I am," she says still laughing.

"Riiiiight," I continue being sarcastic which only makes her laugh more.

After a while she giggles and stops at a red light. My mom watches me for a moment. "I love you Reese's Monkey," she mumbles. Reese's Monkey is my nickname from the family. I've has it since I was little.

"I love you too, ma." I say smiling she smiles back and presses on the gas as the traffic light turns green.

We drive on, both of us are smiling but my smile falters when I see bright lights heading towards us, as a truck weaves onto our side of the road. By the looks of it the driver is drunk.

"MOM!" I scream at the top of my lungs.

There's a sudden jolt, a sharp pain, then darkness consumes me.

Chapter 7

I open my eyes but my vision is blurry, so I blink furiously until it clears. I'm upside down in a car. I look to my right and in the drivers side is my mom. There's lots of blood and I know it's not mine.

Her head is bleeding and she's passed out. I go to shake her shoulder but as soon as my fingers touch her skin I pull away. She's cold, somethings terribly wrong. I feel a sharp pain in my leg and I look down. I close my eyes at the sight.

A large piece of glass sticks up from my left thigh and it's surrounded by blood. My window is shattered so I unbuckle my seat belt and begin to climb out. With my hands on the door of the car I push myself out in my upside down position. I see a road up the hill as I sit in the ground, in the dark. I stand up using the car to steady myself, and hobble up to the road.

I reach the top and look down to my leg in the street light. I put my hands on the glass and hiss as I slowly rip it out. The warm blood runs down my leg and I throw the glass to the ground. I look up to see headlights in the distance. Relived, I make my way to the center of the road and put my hands up to wave them down. Luckily, the car pulls over to the side of the road.

I begin to walk over and my knees are becoming weak as I do so. The cars door opens and a person hurries out and slams the door shut, running over to me. I stand there in the dark with my head down as the person reaches me. "Are you okay?" The person asks. It's a guys voice, it's low and quite familiar actually.

I look up and my eyes lock with blue similar ones.

"Reese?" Graham asks. my breathing is heavy and I blink slowly. I feel light-headed.

I point down the hill and we both look over. My moms car is upside down, the front is smashed, the windshield is shattered, and the passengers window is broken with glass lying around it on the ground. To say our car is demolished is an understatement. A little below my car is a grey truck lying on it's side. Graham's sharp intake of breath is enough to snap me out of my daze.

My mom is down there in that car and she's hurt, if not dead, I need to help her. My eyes widen in realization as I begin to walk down the hill. I get about four steps before his hand is wrapped around my arm.

I turn to look at him and he's just shaking his head. "My moms down there, let me go." I plead.

"What can you do? Just stay here and call for an ambulance," he reasons.

"I don't have my phone," I say. If I don't get down there soon she's going to die, if she hasn't already.

"I do, come here." He pulls me to his car.

"No I need to h-help my mom," I stutter breathlessly and move away from him. "She's hurt and-" My knees give in and I close my eyes, letting out a breath as I fall. I feel a pair of strong arms wrap around my waist before I hit the ground. I'm lifted up slowly to my feet again.

"Can you stand?" Graham questions his arms still holding me tight.

"Yeah I'm fine," I mumble and he lets go, watching me warily. I stumble and automatically his arms are around me again.

"Sure you are," he says. He puts one of his arms under mine, across my back. Then the other around the back of my knees as he lifts me up and carries me bridal style to his car, placing me in the passenger seat as he climbs into the drivers.

He pulls out his phone and dials 911. "911, what's your emergency?"

"There's been an accident," I listen as Graham explains what he knows.

I feel as if I'm floating and sharp pains shoot up and down my left leg. I put my hand over the wound and apply pressure to try and stop the bleeding. It's not that bad, I've had worse but it still hurts. It stings as I touch it and my breath becomes shaky.

That seems to grab Graham's attention, unfortunately. I don't want him to do anything about it, he needs to leave it alone. I glance over at him and his eyes are locked on my leg. I can feel the warm liquid in between my fingers, making it's way over top of them. "Let me see," he demands.

"Does blood make you squeamish?" I ask seriously.

"No, just let me see." He reaches for my hand to pull it away.

"Okay, but just know that when you pass out it's not my fault," I say with a small smile trying to lighten the mood and he faintly returns it. Then reaches for my hand again, "Just leave it."

He doesn't listen and he pulls my hand away from the wound. His jaw clenched and he closes his eyes as he takes a breath. "Keep pressure on it," he says. I just roll my eyes and put my hand back on it.

My vision darkens around the edges and my breathing becomes heavy again. I lay my head on the car door and look in the mirror. My face is pale and the bags under eyes are dark. I'm sweating badly.

"Are you hot?" Graham asks.

"No," I breathe a laugh. "I'm cold."

"But you're sweating."

"Yeah, I feel like a fat man that just got out of the gym after 3 hours of nonstop exercise." I squirm uncomfortably in the seat. He chuckles and shakes his head at me. "I hope you don't mind but I'm getting blood all over your car."

"It's fine," he says quietly. Just then I heard the faint sound of a siren in the distance. I jump out of the car and Graham follows, walking over to me and holding me in place by my arm.

When the police and ambulance arrive, they go over the hill and get my mom out. One man looked to be middle aged, he looked at his partner and shook his head. Oh no.

A slightly younger man with blonde hair and brown eyes approached me. I was sitting in the back of the ambulance with a female that looked about 30 with light brown hair pulled into a low pony tail working on my leg and Graham was sitting beside me. He was watching the girl intently as she cleaned out the gash. "You need stitches," she says to me.

"Mrs. Fode?" The man addresses me.

"Yes?" I respond.

"I'm officer Menna but you can just call me Andy," he says. "I'll be working on the case."

"What case?" I ask.

"Look we need to get her to the hospital and get her stitches," the woman working on my leg interjects.

"Okay, I'll talk to you after you're done." He soon leaves and I pull myself up in the truck.

I've been at the hospital for an hour or so. "There, all done." The woman says finishing up on my leg. "Take it easy and don't put to much stress on that leg."

"Gotcha," I sit up and walk over to the door. She gives me some abnormally large bandages and medical tape for the wound. I exit and Andy finds me on my way to the desk to pay.

"Reese," he says.

"What case?" I say getting straight to the point.

He sighs, looking like he was having an inner battle. "It's been classified as a hit and run, the other person in the crash wasn't in the truck or anywhere near the sight but we did find small blood spots which led us to believe that they're hurt. There was also empty beer cans on the floor of the vehicle so the person was more than likely intoxicated."

"Where's my mom? They said she wasn't here," I ask confused.

"Your mother didn't make it, she was killed on impact so there was no pain." His voice laced with sympathy as he assured me. "I'm sorry Reese." He gave me a pitiful look.

My mom is dead? What, how could this happen? She was pregnant, what happened to the baby? "What about the baby she was carrying?" I asked as my eyes became glassy.

"The baby passed with her, I'm truly sorry." He sounded so hurt. The tears flooded my eyes and I collapsed onto the floor. Andy wrapped his arms around me in attempt to comfort me as I cried silently with a hand over my mouth.

I arrived home and tell Jay about what had happened and I must admit this is the first time I've ever saw him cry. I feel bad but I can't help it, even if he's a terrible person he lost his wife and a child. He just proved to me that he did love my mom and that he does have a heart. He went up to his bedroom and locked the door.

I go to my room and begin to rearrange the furniture. I don't like the color. I run upstairs to my old room and find all the plastic wraps for the furniture from the last time we painted the house. I go down stairs and lay all the plastic on the couch and put the few things I took out if my boxes back in. On the top of one of my boxes was a picture. It was the one I used to have in my dresser. I slowly pick it up examining it. It was from a carnival when I was thirteen. My aunt is on the left of me with one arm around my shoulder. My mom is in the right of me with one arm around me, towering over me and slightly taller than my aunt. I'm in the middle with both if their arms draped on my tiny shoulders. We're all smiling but the biggest smile belongs to my mother. Her dimples show prominently and her short brown hair falls just below her shoulders freely. She looks so happy. How could she just leave me like this? How can she be gone?

Anger flares through me as I throw the picture at the wall, shattering the glass. I back up against the nearest wall, diagonal from the broken glass, sliding down the wall. I bring my knees to my chest and then put my head on my knees letting a sob escape my lips. I gasp for air and cry leaning against the wall mumbling absolute nonsense.

This is my fault. If I hadn't let her drive we'd both be here right now. Why did I live? I should have been the one to die, not her. This is all my fault.

I need to get my mind of this and keep busy. So I pull out a book and start to read. After a couple hours I feel drowsy, my eyelids are becoming heavy from crying. "I'm sorry, I guess I just destroy everything. I'm sorry I destroyed you. I always thought that Jay was the monster but I was wrong. I am, I'm destruction and I break everything I touch. The thing that sucks the most is that I can't take it back, I can't bring you back. So that means I have to let go. All I wanted was to protect you and my baby sister or brother, but I couldn't. I failed." I say hoarsely. "I'm not going to fail with Cameron, Adrienne, Graham, and Brianna. I refuse, I will protect them. From Jay and myself included. I'm sorry I couldn't do the same for you. I'm going to bring up my grades and I'm going to make you proud. I won't let you down this time, I promise. I have to let you go now as best I can, I'm going to try. Goodbye mom." I finish with a sore throat.

I am destruction, I'm like fire. I may start small but I will spread fast and demolish anything in my path, and I don't even mean to.

Goodbye mom, I love you.

CHAPTER 8

I finally went back to school on Friday. I tried to convince myself not to go because there's only one more day in the week and there's really no sense in going but I needed to get my mind off of certain things and I needed to tell Cameron and Adrienne about what had happened, considering I completely closed my self off from the world over the past few days, more than usual.

I've spent my week watching horror movies, reading books, sculpting, indulging myself in food, and thinking. About my mom, my friends and family and by that I mean my aunt, and even Graham. Why? Well I have absolutely no idea. I have had a lot of spare time.

I walk into my history class hold my books tightly to my chest. I keep my head down and shuffle to the back. I set through the whole class unable to focus as the teacher babbles on. I hear the bell ring. So I stand up to leave but my name was called and I look up. "Would you stay after class, I need to speak with you." Mr. Wong asks looking hesitant. I didn't do anything this time, I promise.

I stand in front of his desk and he looks around the room waiting for everyone to leave. The last person out is Graham. I didn't even know he was here. Granted I haven't been paying attention to anything. He gave me a confused look as he stopped at the door but I nodded telling him to go. He walked out with that same confused expression on his face.

"Ms. Fode?" Mr. Wong grabs my attention.

"Is this about make up work?" I wonder aloud.

"No," he says beginning to tap his red pen on the desk.

"Are my grades slipping?" I ask nervously. This is history and I suck at history so I'm pretty sure I have a C at the most.

"No, no, nothing like that. You still have the same grade as before," he reassures fidgeting. "Its about your mom."

"Of course it is," I mumble, rolling my eyes, and turning on my heel to exit.

"I was just going to recommend seeing a therapist or talking to someone about it." He rushes and I stop in my tracks. What?

I do not need to see a therapist. I don't even know how he found out, I haven't told anyone yet. I'm so tired of people. Why can't they just mind their own business and leave me alone! It's my moms death, it's my problem not theirs. If this is starting already I'm just going to leave. You do have to come back sometime and it's not going to get any better.

Ugh!

"I don't need a therapist, it's not like I'm crazy or anything." I snap turning to him once again.

"No but it's tough to go through, especially when you're with her when she passed." He said softly, looking at me like I was broken.

"Well aren't I supposes to deal with that?" I say more of a statement than question.

"Yes but sometimes it's easier to talk to someone," he says.

"How would it be easier to talk to someone who doesn't give a crap about your situation." I exasperated, I have to stop showing emotion.

"Just think about it, okay. I even have a card for one of the better ones if you'd like." He tries but it doesn't work.

"No." I say monotonous and walk out the door but I hear him call something.

"If you change your mind I'm here."

I'm not going to. I think to myself as I trudge down the hall.

My second period was literature and when I enter I see Cameron and he seems extremely chipper. He takes a seat beside me and pokes my side. I immediately move away with a hint of a smirk on my lips. He smiles brightly. "Why weren't you here? Ad has been talking my ear off with non-stop complaints," he groaned.

"I need to tell you something but I want to tell you all together because I don't want to say it or be bombarded with a billion questions more than once today," I say looking at him.

He seems to realize my serious tone and expression and he nods silently getting up to move to the seat in front of me as the teacher walks in. We had switched seats and Cameron sat in front of me and Graham and Brianna sat on either sides of me.

I stare at the ground blankly, slumped in my seat and I can feel Graham's eyes on me.

"Ms. Fode can you tell me what point of view this is?" Mr. Ford calls out and I look up. He's standing by the board with a paragraph projected on it. The lights were on so it made it slightly difficult to see. I squinted to see and read the first sentence. I didn't catch it, it landed in a puddle beside me. I read it silently to my self.

I then look to the teacher, "First person." I say rubbing my eye.

"How do you know?" He asks raising an eyebrow.

"Because it uses words like I and me," I only elaborated a little. It's not like I'm stupid or anything I just don't like to do work. It's not worth my time. I usually copy off of Cameron and Adrienne. Or I just don't do my homework. I'm good with test and quizzes because I already know a lot of the stuff we go over but I don't try. Besides this is basic stuff.

"Okay, good just pay attention." He says moving back to the board and continuing his lesson. Fat chance.

I look back at the ground but I can still feel Graham looking at me. I look up at him and I was right he's been watching me. That's kind of creepy.

"What?" I ask.

"N-nothing but we need to get to work on that volcano." He says clearing his throat.

"Why haven't you been working on it?" I ask with wide eyes.

"I have but the teacher didn't exactly approve if my art skills and made me start over. This time she said you have to help," he continues. "But since you haven't been here she's given us more time to do it. It's due Monday."

"Please tell me we don't have to do the whole project this weekend." I plead.

He laughs a little. "No, I already have the design."

"Okay good but where are we going to meet at?" I ask.

"Well I was hoping your house." He says running a hand through his hair. My eyes widen and I shake my head frantically. "Please, my moms holding this dinner thing and she told me I couldn't make a mess or anything. I'm not even aloud to have any friends over. Can we please just do it at your house?" He finishes in a pleading tone.

I seriously doubt Jay will be there but if he is then it could end bad. I remember the time I had Adrienne over he didn't do anything because my mom was there but he yelled at me and we stayed in my room until she had to leave the next day. We were both twelve when that happened. So imagine what it would be like if it were now and I had a boy over. The outcome would probably be fatal.

I live in the basement now. He doesn't come down there so this may work, but if Graham gets hurt I'll never forgive myself. Jay won't be there tonight or all day tomorrow. He won't even be back until Sunday. He's working on a house that's far away so he's staying in a hotel all weekend. This could work. Besides I have to paint the basement so once we finish the project I can make him help me.

"Okay we can do it at my house, on one condition." I say smiling.

"What is it?" He asks cautiously.

"You have to help me paint my basement when we're done," I state.

"How many spray cans is that going to take?" He asks making a face. I just glare at him and smack one of his broad shoulders. Wow, he is really muscular!

He smirks, "I'll help."

"Thanks," I say glancing at the clock. It's almost time to leave.

"Ms. Fode, Mr. Winters would you care to share with the class?" The teacher asks loudly.

"Nope." I state nonchalantly.

Mr. Fords face seems to redden and he starts to yell. "I will not have you disrupting my class anymore this year Ms. Fode."

I just look at him. He starts to yell again but he's cut off by the bell. Saved by the bell. I think to myself as I wave to Mr. Ford and exit the classroom. His face looked like a fire truck.

Now it's time for my favorite class of the day, art. I really enjoy art, I even work on it at my house. I have clay and molds and an airbrush, but I need a new one. I need new paint as well.

As I enter my class Mrs. Platt was sitting at her desk and when she saw me a smile broke out on her face. She doesn't know, that's a good sign. "Glad to have you back, Reese." She says as I take my seat. This is the only class I sit in the front in. I actually pay attention in this class.

"Glad to be back." I respond, "lets get started."

She smiles brightly and starts the lesson. I listen intently the entire class and then the bell rings. I stand up, collect my things, and walk out.

The next class is gym and all the Juniors have this together. Once I get changed and do my exercises, the teacher announces that we're playing dodgeball. This is going to be so much fun! Note heavy sarcasm.

Adrienne and I get on the same team and we play the game. We do what the tittle says and dodge the balls, that's all we do. I'm not laying a hand on one of those things unless I'm giving it to someone else, they're evil. Ad and I just talk most of the class. It's only until we're the last ones in that we have to play. She throws the red ball and gets Nick Sanches out. Then she purposely tosses it and Graham catches it. Now I'm the only one in, great. "Traitor," I mutter as she passes.

She chuckles at me. "You can't do it." She does that a lot.

"Jerk," I mumble but she heard it and chucked again.

I move around the balls that are thrown and throw the balls aimed at peoples feet so they can't catch them. After just three minutes of this I give up and walk up to the line. "Hit me," I demand and Graham laughs shaking his head as he walks up to me and touches my stomach with the blue ball.

"New game." Mr. Pollid yells and I groan.

"It's not that bad," Graham says.

"Yes it is. This is physical labor." I exasperate.

Graham just laughs at me. "You've got this," he chants.

"Ha ha you're hilarious." I say sarcastically and he chuckles. Then his closest friend, Nick Sanches, walks up to him and whispers something in his ear. I turn away and walk back to Adrienne.

After gym I go to lunch and sit down at the table that my friends are at. I know I have to tell them and I want to get it over with, so here it goes, "hey guys."

"Hey," Brianna says moving over so I can sit down beside Adrienne. Cameron is eyeing me suspiciously.

"I have something to tell you guys." I swallow hard.

Cameron stays quiet, watching me intently. "A couple days ago I was on my way to the hospital with my mom because she was pregnant and she thought there was something wrong, but there wasn't. On the way back home a car ran over onto our side of the road and we crashed." I hear Adrienne's gasp. "We went over the side of the road and I passed out for a while but at least I'm still alive." I let out a humorless laugh. "Mom died on impact. I shouldn't have let her drive, but I did and now she gone. That's why I missed school." Cameron gets up and moves around the table to comfort me. the next thing I knew I had three pairs of arms wrapped around me tightly.

"I'm so sorry Reese." Cam says quietly.

"Don't apologize," I say.

The bell rings and it's time to go back to class, science. I sigh as I collect my books and head to class. I sit beside Graham as the other students show their projects.

Ms. Jo looks to us. "You guys can show you're project Monday then we'll get to work on the second one."

"You got it," I reply just as the bell rings.

"Your house this weekend right?" Graham reminds as we exit.

"Yes, Saturday morning. You pick the time." I say walking to my math class.

"Um how's ten?" He asks.

"Tens perfect," I say entering the class and taking my seat.

I go through math then study hall and then go to my locker go get my bag. As I mentioned before I don't do homework and the stuff I did have I completed in the last class then finished out the period drawing.

I stuff my books in my locker and grab my bag. I close the locker door to see a creepily grinning Cameron. I gasp then breathe deeply leaning my forehead against the door.

"Let's go." he says grabbing my arm and hauling me down the corridor.

"Where are we going?" I groan, staggering as I walk.

"You'll see," he says.

"You're not going to kidnap and torture me are you?" I ask jokingly.

"Normally kidnaping someone is forceful. I would know." He plays along.

"This is hardly willing," I smirk.

He just laughs and pulls me outside to a bright red colored Saturn Ion. It's Adrienne's car. She's already in the drivers seat and Brianna is in the passengers. Cameron picks me up and tosses me in then gets in after me, scooting me over a little.

"What is this?" I ask in a weird tone.

"You need a pick me up." Ad says simply and Brianna giggles as she takes off with a jolt.

CHAPTER 9

The image attached is Reese's dress.

"Kidnapping is illegal, Ad." I say as she takes a sharp turn. "Remember you were planning on kidnapping Connor Franta." I continue jokingly.

"I remember when the two of you got arrested for trespassing and called me to get my parents to bail you out because you didn't want to tell your own." Cameron recalls looking between the two of us accusingly as we both laugh. Brianna looks at us in bewilderment which only makes us laugh more.

"Just tell me where we're going," I groan.

"We're almost there just shut up." Ad says rolling her eyes.

"Oh I know where we're going." I say, suddenly realizing that we're on the way to the mall.

"What how?" Ad asks confused.

"You've dragged me here enough to know the way. I even know a shortcut." I say giving her a knowing look.

"You've got me there." She says nodding.

Brianna just laughs at the two of us and shakes her head.

"I never did here about your trip to the mall with Holly and her brainwashed bitches. How'd it go?" I ask directing my attention toward Brianna.

She shrugs. "It wasn't that bad but she's annoyingly chipper and really loud." She brings her finger up to her ear and moves it back and forth rapidly. "I think I went deaf."

We all laugh and Ad asks, "did you pick a dress?"

"Kind of, I mean it's pretty but not really my taste." Brianna explains to us.

"Then why'd you buy it?" Cam asks scrunching up his nose and furrowing his brows.

She looks up to the roof of the car and mumbles something along the lines of, "I didn't want to but she made me. Insisting that it would look amazing."

"How much was it," I ask.

"It was actually one of the cheaper ones and it wasn't that much. Around five hundred," she shrugs.

"Five hundred!" Cam shrieks.

"I wouldn't even pay anywhere over ten dollars for a dress." I murmur to myself.

"I don't really like it." She says looking at me.

"Oh don't worry we'll help you pick a new dress and we can get you one too, Reese." Ad says smirking at me in the mirror.

She loved to take me shopping. Every time we would leave a store we would have at least three more bags, just from her. I don't like to shop that much. Ad doesn't like to shop unless it's for her and I feel the same way. I'll go if it's for me or her. Other than that I don't want to go. I also hate dresses and she knows it. She has great style though.

"I don't have any money." I lie. Cam and Ad look at me with tired expressions.

"You must think we're stupid." Cam says.

"I'm your best friend. I know you keep money in your bag every-where you go, even if it's just to my house." Ad points out.

I just sigh and lay my head back in the seat. She smiles tri-umphantly at my silence, taking it as a win. She has an obsession with winning and is extremely competitive.

"What else are we going to do, other than go dress shopping for all of you?" Cameron asks blinking slowly as Adrienne grinned at him.

"Oh, hey." I shout gaining jumps and looks of shock from Brianna and Cam. "We could go watch a movie." I suggested.

"Fine with me," Cam shrugs.

"Yeah, which one?" B asks.

"We can decide when we get there." Cam says just as Ad parks, turning of the engine.

"What type of movie?" Cam asks us all.

"A scary one," Ad and I say simultaneously. Then look at each other strangely, chuckling.

"They are evil!" Cam exclaims, extending his whole arm just to point a finger in our direction.

We all laugh walking into Sears. "Why did we come in this store?" B asks.

"There's more parking space outside of here than anyplace else. She parks there every time we come here." I explain. B just nods as we walk out of Sears.

After a while we make our way to the theater and take a look at the choices.

"What about spongebob?" Cam asks and we all shrug. "Really you two are willing to watch a movie that's not scary?" He continues, looking between Ad and I.

"Of course, it's spongebob." Ad says as if he should already know it, and I agree.

He just says; "Okay when's it on next?"I point at the next showing. Six pm. he nods and looks at his watch. "It's only five thirty. We can get something to eat after the movie and dress shopping."

Cam had came with us to the mall before so he was used to being pulled around and asked his opinion on things a lot, but he never once objected.

"We're not going to get out of here until late, are we?" B asks me.

"Probably not." I say. "We're here with Adrienne and she'll shop until she drops, literally. She'll end up making Cameron drive us home and she'll fall asleep in the back seat." I smiled at the fact that, that had happened once before. She slapped me once we got home and I tried to wake her.

She chuckles, pulling out her phone, "I need to text Graham and tell him I won't be back until late. Plus since I'm getting a new dress I want his opinion on it"

"Are you sure he's going to like you getting another dress?" I ask. B and I are walking side by side with Cam and Ad in front of us doing the same. He turns to ask her something and she shakes her head at him so he pulls the pouting face and she just looks at him. He stomps and continues walking and she follows shaking her head as she laughs at him.

B shrugs and locks her phone putting it in her pocket. "He already told me he didn't like the other dress because it's too reveling."

"Well then you're set," I say. "Come on, she just turned into a store and we don't have an hour to spend in it,"

B laughs as we follow her. It's a candle store. So I'm guessing she needs to buy her mom a present or something. She and Cam are smelling candles and comparing them. "Why are we in here?" I ask

"I forgot to get my mom a birthday present so I decided to get her one now." Ad shrugs before asking me which of the candles smelled better. How did I know? Eventually she just decides on the cherry one and we leave, heading to the theater again for the movie because Ad managed to kill twenty minutes on candle debating.

We watched the movie, occasionally throwing popcorn in the older woman's hair that was in front of us. We were the only people our age in the theater. I wonder why? We passed the popcorn back and forth until Ad decided we couldn't have anymore and kept it for herself. The movie was good and Cam must have been enjoying it to from the gasps and laughs he let throughout the movie.

Once the movie was over we decided to go dress shopping. Ad had a special store in mind and we wandered around the mall in search for it but when we finally found it she didn't like any of the dresses in it. So we went into another I don't know the name of.

We looked around the store going through dresses of all varieties. Cam just sat on the bench outside of the changing rooms waiting for us. He already knew what he was going to have to do so he waited for us to pick dresses we liked so he could basically judge us.

Immediately B found a dress she liked but she wanted options so she looked for a couple more. Ad had at least three dresses when she ran into the changing rooms. I, on the other hand, just roamed around the store. I had no idea what I wanted, nor did I like any of the dresses I saw. So, I just joined Cam on his bench.

B came out in her first dress. You could tell she loved it and it looked amazing on her. It was a dark blue with a black ribbon around the waist. Flower patterned black lace starts at the ribbon and flows down the dress, ending just above the knees. She spun around in it. "What do you think?" B asked looking to me and Cam.

"You look amazing!" I exclaim.

She looked at herself in the mirror and smiled. "Thank you. I honestly love it. I'm not even going to try the others on. I want this one."

I smile at her and Cameron is still looking at her. "You do look amazing." he said nodding.

She smiled at him and then handed me her phone. "Could you take a picture of me, I need to get Graham's okay?"

I snap the picture and she sends it to her brother mumbling a thanks.

Then Ad came out in a bright red, floor length gown. A sparkling pattern swirled around her entire body. She walked out looking a unsure. Cam shook his head and she rolled her eyes him. "You're bright," I pointed out and she scurried back into the changing room.

Minutes later she came out in a blood red dress with a gem belt around the waist. It was strapless and flowed down to her lower thigh in layers. It wasn't pouffy though, it was a really pretty dress. She looked gorgeous!

"You've got my vote." I told her. She seemed to like this one as well. She looked to Cam and he smiled at her nodding his head. He really hasn't said much in the past twenty minutes. I wonder if something's wrong.

After the girls got back into their clothes and put the other dresses on a hanger in a bin, Ad came up to her. "Where's your dress?" She asked.

"Oh, I'm not getting one." I smile sweetly at her and she glares back at me.

"Yes you are." She says reaching to fix my hair and I flinch but she doesn't seem to notice.

I flinch a lot. I can't really help it though. I'm just glad no one notices.

"I don't like any of the dresses." She just sighs at my response.

"You don't like any dresses at all." she states dragging me along to find a dress.

I see one hanging in a corner and I wander over to it as Ad rambles on about one of the other dresses.

I walk up to it and take it off the hook, inspecting it. It's simple so I go try it on with Ad in tow. She waits patiently for me to come out. When I do she smiles at me. "You look stunning!" Ad exclaims. B was nodding her head frantically in agreement.

I looked at myself in the mirror. The dress was simple. It was white with a black ribbon around the waist and black lace formed vine and flower patterns creeping up the side. It ended just above my knee like the other girls dresses did and it was strapless. I actually like this dress.

"You can't wear that." Cameron says and I look at him in the mirror.

"Why?" I ask.

"Yeah, she looks jaw dropping." Ad says, crossing her arms.

"That's the problem. She looks stunning." Cam responds confusing me. "There will be guys all over you." he continued waving his arms in the air. I laugh at him. "It's going to be hard to watch you all." he huffed.

I smiled widely and engulfed him in a hug and he returned. I don't hug often but when I do you should savor it because it only happens once in a blue moon.

I take the dress off and we all pay for them and then leave. Cam keeps whining about being hungry so I told Ad to stop at a restaurant. We went to Cheddars because Cameron was screaming it. After we ate we were on our way home. Cameron was driving and

I ended up in the front passengers seat with the other two girls passed out in the back. I knew this would happen again.

Cam and I laughed and reminisced the entire way home. First, we dropped off Brianna and then Cameron. So a very sleepy and grouchy Adrienne drive me home.

"Goodnight." she said drowsily.

"Night, Ad." I replied and watched as she drove off.

The day really got my mind off of my mom and everything. As I entered the house I couldn't help but smile. My friends are the best and I wont ever take them for granted.

I walk into the kitchen to grab some snacks and my step dad is at the counter.

"What are you doing back so late?" He asks irritated.

"I went out with friends." I stated getting a water from the fridge and setting my dress down on the back of my chair.

"What's that?" He asks looking to the grey bag behind me.

"My homecoming dress." I say, this is almost a normal conversation.

"Whatever, you need to clean the house my mom is coming over next weekend and this place is a dump." he says getting up and throwing his beer away missing the trash, it lands on the floor.

"Okay could you at least try to keep the house clean." I mumble rolling my eyes.

"What did you just say?" He asks, anger clear in his tone, and now the almost conversation is lost.

"All I said was that you should try and keep the house clean." I look to him. "I cleaned it Tuesday and it's already littered with cans and trash." I explain.

"It's not my job to clean. It's yours. It used to be your moms responsibility but she left me." he growled.

"She didn't leave you, Jay she died." I say shaking my head.

"It was your fault! She would still be alive if it wasn't for you!" he yelled, balling his fists.

I knew it was my fault but I didn't want to say that to him and I felt the need to defend myself, as always. "How was it my fault? I wasn't the one driving." I retaliated.

"Why did you make it?" He sneered, avoiding my question. I stayed silent and he moved towards me. "Now I'm left with you to take care of. I have to adopt you." he says disgusted.

"Adopt me?" I ask cautiously.

He smirked slightly. "Daddy dearest doesn't want you. He doesn't want anything to do with you anymore. He's giving up visitation and your moms dead so she can't keep you. I wasn't going to adopt you initially. My mom said that I should and now she's practically forcing me to."

My chest feels like is collapsing. The room seems to be closing in. My dad is leaving me with him and my moms dead. He's going to be my adoptive father.

"Do the dishes, I'm going to bed." he says walking away but freezes when he hears what comes out of my mouth before I could even stop it.

"No." I say, not daring to turn and face him.

He didn't take my defiance as bad as I'd thought. He slowly approached me from behind and slammed my head to the counter and then yelled "do them," before heading upstairs. Normally defiance would end up bloody. I guess he's in a good mood.

"There's going to be a mark there," I mumble doing the dishes. After I'm done I take my bags and go down stairs. I put my stuff away then lay down on the couch slowly drifting off to sleep.

CHAPTER 10

I wake up in the morning with a bit of a headache. It's not bad, it's just annoying. I look at the clock and see that it's only six in the morning. Graham's coming over at ten, so I can get some stuff done. I trudge upstairs and into the kitchen.

I make some coffee. Sitting at the counter, I drink it. Then put the dish in the sink. I go back down to my room, or rather little apartment. I walk past the fridge and everything and into the bathroom. Sure it's small but it works. I take a shower. Once I'm done I step out and dry off. walking into the living room, which is also where I sleep, I pull out a baggy Rolling Stones band t-shirt and a pair of ripped up jeans. After dressing I decide to just pull my hair up in a messy bun, even though it's still wet because I don't like to dry my hair. Then I tie a dark blue bandana around my head.

I look to the clock and it says 9:06. So, I put the plastic over everything. The tv, dresser, etc. The couch is the only thing that's not covered. I made sure to put my drawings under the coffee table in front of the couch to where Graham won't see them. Looking around the room, I'm pleased with what I've accomplished. Once he comes in here he'll probably think I'm a freak. I have a large, see-through cabinet lining the wall. It holds most of my art supplies. Beside it is a shelf, it holds my molds and stuff. I have an interest in special effects makeup. Like the monsters in movies and stuff. I'm good at it and I love to do it. I have the stuff I've worked on and completed in my art room. I just haven't been able to take the rest of my stuff in there yet.

I gave Graham directions on how to get to my house and I told him to come around the back because that's where the door to the basement is. Shortly before ten I hear a knock at the door so I turn around and he was standing there awkwardly. I waved for him to come in and he opened the door. As he entered he looked around the place.

"I covered everything up so we wouldn't get paint on it." I explained noticing his confusion.

He stopped and looked at my wall, the one with all the art and face molds. He hasn't been here two minutes and he's already weirded out.

I walked over to him and took his bag setting it beside the table. I sat down in the couch and he was still standing, looking around. Soon he sits down beside me. "Lets get to work." he says. He pulls out his ideas and drawings. They aren't that bad, but they aren't that good either. He shows me what he wants to do and then I stand up and walk away. He watches me confusedly. "Where are you going?"

"I'll be right back." I say over my shoulder. I walk into my art room and grab some clay. I walk back and set it on the plastic covered table. Then, I walk over to the cabinet and pull out a few tools. My airbrush, some paint brushes, and paint. I set them down on the table as well. He looked at me for a minute just smiling. "What?" I ask.

"Nothing." he said still smiling.I gave him a weird look and sat back down. "How do we do this?" He asks and I facepalm myself. He just chuckles.

"We sculpt the volcano and then paint it." I say obviously. Then I take the cover off the clay and take off as much as I think we need. Graham just watches me.

I pound it with my hand until I think it's at the thickness I need. I continue to make it rugged. After it looks the way I want, I take one of the tools and begin to make a crack down the center of it. I'm focusing on it as I make it look real.

I turn to face Graham and he's watching me. I hand him the tool and he holds it like he doesn't know what to do with it.

"Finish this while I go and get some things from the cabinet." I say and he looks to the sculpt then back to me.

He nods and I walk away. I gather some small rock like things and walk back over. He still sitting there just looking at the volcano. I laugh and take the tool back. I carve the rest of the crack and smaller ones coming off of the larger. Then I get my airbrush and hook it up. "Can you paint?" I ask him, jokingly.

He smiles at me and takes the paint brush with a jerk which makes me flinch. Luckily, he doesn't notice. I show him the color to paint with and watch as he does so messily, but it still looks good. After he's done, I take my airbrush and touch it up a bit. Then paint a faint red line over the black through the crack acting as lava. I let him place the rocks. Finally, we're are finished.

Graham looks at it in astonishment."It looks so real." he said.

"It looks presentable." I say nodding.

He looks at me in bewilderment. "It looks amazing. It's defiantly the best one in the class. You did excellent."

"Thanks." I murmur. "Now we paint my basement, but we need to wash first." I say laughing at our hands. I grab his arm and pull him off the couch to the bathroom. We're covered in clay and paint up to our elbows. Well I am, he only has it to his forearm because he didn't do very much. We clean up and dry off.

I go to leave but he grabs my arm and I stop looking at him with confusion. He pulls me closer to him. Is he going to hit me? My heart hammers in my chest. "You have some on your face." He says running his thumb over my cheek bone then wiping it on his pants. My cheek is all tingly and I wipe it more. "It's gone." he says. My heart rate slows because I should have known he wasn't going to hit me. But I can't get over the tingly feeling in my cheek.

"Thanks," I murmur. He nods and turn around walking the other way, hiding my blush. As I enter the living room I open the paint and turn to hand hima brush. He takes it and we paint. I can still feel heat on my cheek where his thumb had been.

After a while we manage to paint most of the lower layer. I reach up and try to paint higher but I'm not tall enough. Graham comes over and paints it for me and I smile in return.

We finish after about three hours and it's only five in the afternoon. "Do you have to leave yet?" I ask curiously.

"No I don't have to leave until around midnight," he shrugs.

"Want to watch a movie or something?" I ask him.

"Yeah, what do you have?"

"My movies are under the tv in that drawer." I say. "I'll be right back." I continue.

I hear him mumble an "okay" as I leave to the bathroom. Once I'm in there I see myself in the mirror. My bun has held up surprisingly and I'm only wearing mascara. I use the restroom and then wash my paint flecked hands. I adjust my dark blue bandana then go back out to the living room.

Graham sits on the couch looking through a tablet. There were two movies on the table. Both were scary, I had some comedies in there but I guess he's a horror movie fan like me. Well that and there wasn't much to chose from, the majority of my movies are scary. The movie on the top was The Wicked and the one under it was silent Hill. Once I got closer I realized what he was looking at. They were my drawings and sculpting ideas. I sat down beside him.

"These are amazing," he said breathlessly. He's probably just trying to make me feel better about them.

"They're old." I said a little panicked. What does he think of me now? No doubt he thinks I'm a freak and won't talk to me anymore. Most of my drawings are found creepy by most people. Why would I care what he thinks of me though?

"They are so detailed and realistic," he notes aloud.

"How about we put that away." I say laughing humorlessly and gently taking the tablet from his hands.

"Why don't you want people to see them?" He asked letting me take the tablet.

I quickly hid it back under the table. "I have let people see them, Adrienne." I say.

He looks at me curiously, studying my face. "Just Adrienne?"

"Yeah, I wasn't planning on showing you and technically I didn't, but you kinda found them," I explain looking down at my hands that are twisted in my lap.

"Why are you hiding them?" He asked shaking his head.

I sigh and run a hand through my hair. "Name my friends."

"Adrienne, Brianna, that Cameron guy, me, uh. I'm sure you have others," he struggled.

"No, I don't and I just met you and Brianna, I came here a while ago and I used to have a friend named Mike but we haven't talked in a while. Other people don't have any friends so I'm happy with what I have." I say and I truly believe that. Other people have it worse than me so I have nothing to complain about. I have people who care about me and I don't deserve that.

"Well why don't you show Brianna?" He asked. I'm looking at the floor now.

"Because she'll run." I mumble, but maybe that's for the best. I like her and she's cool but I don't want to hurt her and eventually I know I will.

"Why would you think that? She would never-" he started but I interrupted him.

"You ask a lot of questions." I breathe a laugh standing up and turning on the television. He just sighs and now it was my turn for the questions, I hate being put on the spot. "Which movie do you want to watch first?"

"Uhh this one," he tosses me The Wicked and I put it in and start it. I walk back over to the couch and sit a bit farther away from him than last time.

We watch the movie and he seems so inch a little bit closer every once in a while. After the movie I go to put the other in, then go back to the couch. I plop down and he sighs. I look at him with confusion and he looks back at me. "I just don't understand why you keep this from everyone," he finally says.

I sigh and pause the movie running a hand through my hair. He looks at me and I stand up and walk in front of him. I hold out my hand shakily. I don't like to be touched or any physical contact. I don't like loud noises or sudden movements either and I know that makes me weak but I can't help it. Like when I grabbed his arm earlier, I didn't like that and I don't know why I did it.

He takes my hand carefully and lightning bolts up my arm and shoots throughout my body. Woah, what just happened? I walk towards the washing machine room and once we enter I head towards the door that leads to my art room. I stop and take a deep breath. This is a big deal for me especially when Adrienne is the only one that knows. Jay knows but only because I live with him. I hide these from everyone because I'm always told they're creepy and they suck and I'll never get anywhere in life. Even by my mom. She is the main reason why I don't show anyone. She never allowed me to.

I open the door and pull him in before turning on the light. His eyes widen a fraction as he takes in the view. My sculptures of monsters and other beings I've created over the past few years line the walls on my shelves. There was a small desk in the corner of the room with a lamp and a notebook on it. Graham walked over and opened it, analyzing my drawings and ideas. I became very insecure about my creations, I walked over to him and closed the book, looking up but straight ahead.

He looks around the room and smiled at me. Wait what? Why is he smiling? I gave him a confused look. He probably thinks I'm deranged. He walks over to my latest creation. It's just a face. It's going to be grey, black, and white. I'm not finished with it yet. It's eyes sink into it's head. It's whole face is long and slender as the mouth is open, extended down and jaw is slightly off set. It looks like it's in pain and it's face is lined with wrinkles. "It's not finished." I said.

"What's this?" He asked looking at a machine in the back, left corner of the room.

"It's a Vacuform, you put something in it to make a mold and the plastic slams down and makes a mold out of it." I say walking over and grabbing a cup. I set the cup upside down then turn it on and hit the button after lowering it down a bit. With a loud smack the plastic comes down on the cup and sucked all the air out to make the mold. When it was done I raised it back up and turned it off.

I moved the cup out of the way, took the plastic out, and showed him. "See, then you just cut it out." I explain.

"Oh," he nods and looks around the room again. "Why don't you show anyone, they're all amazing."

I sigh waking over to the door and leaning on the frame. "I have my reasons," I shrug.

"Care to share?" He asks, raising his eyebrows.

"Nope." I say popping the p. He chuckles softly, shaking his head as he sets the plastic down. After that he walks over to one of the shelves and looks at them. When he reaches the end of this shelf he turns to the corner of the room where another sculpt is. This one is a full body, made only from modeling clay.

I didn't give the face a whole lot of detail. The eyes were x's, there was no nose, and the mouth was sewn shut. The head was tilted to the left. The chest was broad and the arms spiral around the body, coming to a sharp point at the feet. The legs were slightly bent and one foot was in front of the other. The entire sculpt was grey.

Graham looked up at it because it was taller than him by about two feet. "These are astounding." He breathes.

I smile lightly and walk up beside him. I look at the sculpt and put my hands in my back pockets. I can see him looking at me from my peripheral vision. I scrunch my eyebrows together but continue staring at the sculpt. "We can go finish our movie now," I say, finally looking at him.

"Okay," he nods as we walk to the door. He heads to the couch and I stay back and take one last look at my creations before turning off the light and following him. Maybe they're not that bad.

Once I get back to the couch I un-pause Silent Hill and we watch the rest of it then put in another. After that one I look at the clock and realize how late it is.

"When do you have to leave again?" I ask still looking at the clock.

"Around midnight, why?" He asks groggily.

I chuckle and smack his chest. When he looks at me with confusion, I point to the clock on the wall. He groans and rolls over onto the pillow beside him. I chuckle again and stand up, stretching my back. It's two in the morning so I'd say he's a bit late. "Your parentals are going to be worried." I said after my back cracked.

"My parentals?" He asked looking up at me with a smirk playing at his lips.

"That's what I said," I nod, walking over to the light and flicking it on. Light flooded the room and immediately I slammed a hand over my eyes and rubbed them until they got used to the brightness. Graham let out another groan and he stood up to get his bag. He rummaged through it for a minute before pulling out his phone. He quickly dialed a number and put the device up to his ear.

Eventually he hung up and called another number. When that one didn't answer either he turned to me. "Could you drive me to my house?" He asked.

"I don't have a car," I state.

"Well I don't either." he sighed running a hand through his hair then down his face.

"How do you plan on getting home?" I asked raising my brows.

"I don't know," he said as he threw a couple things into his bag.

Well Jay won't be home tonight. He'll probably be back tomorrow night. So, maybe he can stay here. "You can stay here tonight." Wait what? I didn't mean to say that! Crap!

"Are you sure?" He asks.

Well it's already out there now, might as well. We both know your making up excuses so he can stay. "Yeah you can sleep on the couch I'll sleep on the chair." I reason, ignoring the voice in my head.

He nods and I go to get some blankets and pillows. I find a dark blue blanket and a light blue pillow in the washing room. Then, I just get my regular blanket and pillow that I use every night. I walk back and toss him the blue ones. He murmurs a simple "thanks" before making his bed.

"Are you tired?" He asks after the beds are made, and by that I mean we strung out the blankets messily and threw the pillows down.

"Not really," I say. The movement and brightness of the light woke me up.

"Do you want to watch another movie?"

"Sure," I say, lying down on the chair. The chairs angle of the television makes it difficult to see.

Graham walks over to the drawer and picks out a movie. Once he puts it in the DVD player and starts it up, he sits back down on the couch. "You can sit over here if you want. So you can see the movie better." he rushes the last part. Once this movies over I can just go back to the chair.

I go and sit down beside him. I recognize the movie on the screen as The Sacred. "You sure like your scary movies," I laugh.

"This coming from the girl who owns nothing but scary movies," he retaliated.

"There were comedies in there!" I defend myself pointing to the drawer. He laughs and turns back to the movie.

As the movie goes on I can feel myself drifting off to sleep and by the looks of it Graham's headed there too. My vision blurs for a moment and then I was out.

CHAPTER 11

(Graham's POV)

I wake up and I'm hugging something. I'm not sure what it is but it's comfortable. I crack one eye open and realize it's not a something, it's a someone. Reese is in my arms. We must have fallen asleep like this. I remember her falling asleep and I didn't want to wake her, but that's it.

My arms are around her waist and her back is to my chest. She's curled up, so her thighs are brushing my arms. She looks so peaceful and cute. I don't want to move. Wait! No, stop. She's not supposed to be cute! Remember what Nick said! I look up to the clock and see that it's nine. I need to get home.

My parents can't get mad. They didn't answer, neither did my sister and I didn't have a ride home. Besides, they lock the doors after midnight anyways. They have major security problems.

I look back down at Reese. She looks so peaceful and angelic. I've never seen her like this. She's always tense and alert. She flinches a lot. I don't even think she notices half the time, it's just instinct. No normal person would flinch that much. I just pretend not to notice, but I know something's up and I intend to find out what.

Suddenly, my phone rings loudly. Reese stirs in my arms and I reach over the edge of the couch and into my bag quickly declining the call so it doesn't disturb her. After flipping around to face me, she slowly relaxes and cuddles into my chest. I can't help but smile. she balls her fists and puts them on my chest leaning into them. I laugh lightly, I look back at my phone and go to my calls. Holly called again. This is the third time this week! I thought she would get the hint the second time I ignored her. She just won't leave me alone! I mean she's hot, but just how Nick talks about her I can tell he likes her, so he can have her. There are other good looking girls around here. I glance at the clock once again. Wow it's already been a half an hour. My phone goes off again and I answer. "Where are you?" My mother asks automatically.

I quietly respond, "I stayed at Reese's."

"You should have called," she said stubbornly.

"I did," I said lowly still watching Reese to make sure she doesn't wake up. "You never answered."

"Ohh," she drags out and I roll my eyes. "Sorry honey," she finishes.

"Mhm." I say

"What time are you going to be home?"

"I don't know."

"Well I'm making dinner tonight, you can bring your little friend if you'd like." She teases me like she always does.

"You know some how I don't think she'll want to do that," I say.

"Well why not?" She whines and I laugh.

"She's got plans." I lie, well really it's not lying she may have plans.

My mom sighed, "Okay well be home by lunch."

"Will do, love you." I say, hanging up.

Now I can lay like this for a little longer. I smile down at her sleeping face. Her eyes flutter open. "Well apparently not," I mumble. She looks up at me confused. She looks cute when she's confused.

She not cute, I remind myself.

She looks around the room before growling and slamming her head back down. I breathe a laugh. She suddenly tenses again and I realize that my arm is still around her waist. I've noticed she doesn't like to be touched or be too close to people.

I remove my arm and she sets up rubbing her eyes and walking over towards the bathroom. Wow, I thought she was going to slap me. I set up as well and put my phone back in my bag. shortly after she comes back out with her hair still falling out but it still looks good and her eyes were still sleepy. She was wearing a Rolling Stones band shirt! I love The Rolling Stones! Most of her makeup was faded off but she still looked the same.

"Morning," she mumbles.

"Morning," I reply.

"Sorry about falling asleep on you. You should have woke me up I would have moved." She apologizes to me.

"You weren't bothering me." I shrug and smirk. She glares at me and I get slightly scared.

"I'm not in the mood," she growls and I smirk even more. "What time is it?"

"Theres a clock right there." I point to it.

She closes her eyes and sighs, she looks back up to the clock and her eyes go wide. It's only ten now. "What time are you leaving?"

"Um I have to be home by lunch. Wh-" I start but she interrupts.

"Do you want to go home early? I would walk with you," she rushes.

"Sure?" I say more of a question.

"Okay we can stop and get a sandwich or something." She suggests, grabbing her bag and running into the bathroom.

What was that? Is she trying to get rid of me?

She returns and her hair is down and brushed. "Lets go!" She says rushing out the door.

Okay then?

We go out her french doors and head up the small hill. I wondered why we didn't go upstairs, but that's none of my business. Once we reach the top of the hill a truck pulls up. Reese freaks out and shoves me over the hill then runs down after me.

"What the hell?" I ask standing up. I look over at her and her eyes are wide as her chest heaves up and down rapidly. She pulls me over to the back wall of her house and peaks around the corner.

"Sorry," she mumbles softly.

"Are you-" I begin but I'm interrupted for the second time today.

"Shut up," she snaps harshly. I do as she says and keep my mouth shut. "Wait here. Quietly," she reminds me in whisper tone. She slips inside the house and I stand awkwardly outside. After a minute she steps back out, "Okay c'mon."

"What was that?" I asked.

"I don't know what you're talking about." She says, faking innocence.

"You pushed me down the hill!" I exclaimed, gesturing down the hill.

"No, no you tripped over air." She says nodding.

"You're so annoying." I say shaking my head and following her up the hill.

"Really, first you accuse me of pushing you down a hill and now you're calling me annoying," she teases. I can't help but laugh at what she's saying, but something really seems weird. One minute she looks like she's having a panic attack and then next she's calm and joking around.

We walk up to the road and stroll down it, making our way to town. After we go to town we get some subs and finish eating them, she offers to walk with me to my house insisting she has time to kill and I was also in the middle of a story that she has to hear the end to. Once we make it to my house she looks at it wide eyed. Mine is defiantly larger than hers but it's not that big. It's a tan and brown house like hers but bigger in size. It has a large yard and a side walk connected to the driveway.

"Okay bye now." She says smiling and waving then turning in her heel to walk away.

"Wait," I say and she turns around to face me again, waiting for me to continue but I don't. I pull her into a light hug and whisper a 'thanks' in her ear but she stiffens and flinches as soon as my arms are around her.

"Uh yeah," she says awkwardly walking away with her head down and her hands in her back pockets. There's definitely something up with her.

"Mom, I'm home!" I shout as I walk into the house and sit my bag on the living room couch.

"Lunch is almost finished," she called loudly.

"I already ate." I say walking into the kitchen.

"What did you eat?" She asks moving around the counter.

I lean on the island with my arms crossed over my chest. "Just some subs."

"Well for dinner we're having your favorite." She turned with a smile.

"Tacos?" I ask and she nods.

"Can you do me a favor?" My mom asks as she puts the sand-wiches she made on a plate.

"Sure," I reply waiting for her to continue.

"I need you to run over to the neighbors house and give them this." she says handing me a tupperware box filled with cupcakes. "And don't eat any on the way over." She quickly adds pointing a warning finger at me as I grin.

"Which neighbor?"

"The new ones."

"We have new neighbors?" I ask curiously. I wonder who they are.

She nods before responding. "Yeah, they moved into the huge house on the corner beside us."

"You mean the house that no one has lived in for a while?" I ask, tilting my head to the right.

"How'd you know about that?" She looks up at me.

"Nick," I replied. Not needing to know anymore she says oh and I leave to see the new neighbors.

I walk to their front porch and I realize just how big the house actually is. It's almost twice the size of mine! I ring the door bell and wait for an answer. The door opens to a an older looking woman but probably only in her late fifties. She had long blonde hair that was naturally straight and pulled into a pony. She was tall and skinny and wearing a light blue dress with some heels. She looks rich.

"Hello?" She said but it was more of a question.

"Hi, I live over there." I said using my thumb to indicate it. "My family and I just wanted to welcome you to the neighborhood. I brought cupcakes." I said handing the clear box to the woman.

"Oh, thank you young man but we've lived around here for years we just moved into a bigger house on this street. It's supposed to be the biggest house in town." She explains.

"Oh," I said awkwardly.

"I haven't seen you around before. How long have you been here?" She asks.

"A couple months," I say nodding.

"I'm guessing you're still in school."

"Yes mam," I confirmed.

"You most probably know my daughter, Holly Cherish." She says formally.

"Um yeah, I know her." Oh wow, this is Holly's mom. "Well it's nice to meet you but I have to go home."

"You too, young man." She says politely as I walk down the sidewalk hearing the door shut behind me. Okay so Holly's rich and she's my neighbor, great. I step into the house and head straight to my room.

"Dinner!" My mom calls from down stairs.

I trudge down the steps and in to the dining room. On the table were three plates with two tacos on each dish except one. The last one had four tacos on it. My family knows me so well. My father wasn't home, he was at work so we ate without him. My sister was seated at one side of the medium sized circular table and my mom on the other. I sat down in my seat and dug in. The dinner was filled with conversations about school, the neighbors, and many other things. When Brianna found out that we lived next to Holly she slumped in her seat and sighed. I laughed at the action but mom scolded her. Later we all watched television together and had our own little family time, minus my father because he has to work the late shift, but occasionally my mind would wander over to Reese. I wondered what she was doing and if she was spending time with her family. If she even had any, I don't really know very much about her. She just won't tell me anything. She closes herself off from everyone. I'm going to get to know her and she's going to open up to me, I'm sure of it.

CHAPTER 12

(Reese's POV)

I step back into the house and it's already ten at night. I stalled all day long. Going to see Adrienne and then I had dinner with Cameron and spent some time at the rail road tracks before walking back home. As soon as I closed the door behind me a voice sounded from the dining room. "Where have you been? You were gone when I got home too." At least he didn't see Graham and I this morning.

"I was at a friends for a while." I explained myself.

"What friends? You don't have any." He said rudely. I decide not to talk back this time seeing as he already had a slight slur and a Bud-light in his hand. "Anyways, my mother is coming over this weekend and she wants to see you."

I actually like his mom. She's kind and rude all at the same time. She's funny and she always has good stories about her teenage years. She was the polar opposite of her son. "How long will she stay?"

"Until Sunday." He said curtly.

"Okay," I said walking to the basement. He didn't stop me, he just let me go. Maybe his mom can come over every weekend, he seems a lot happier when he knows she's coming or when she's already here.

I step into the basement and set my stuff down on the coffee table. Then my phone goes off. "Hello?" I answer.

"Hey, what's up?" Adrienne asked.

"Nothing, nothing at all." I said sarcastically, smiling to myself.

"I'm not helping you clean up the body this time," she says jokingly.

"No fair!" I play along.

"I'm not cleaning up your mess if I didn't get to join in the fun." She says like I should already know it. "Okay now seriously, do you wanna go to the mall this weekend?"

"I can't, Jay's mom is coming down, she's staying until Sunday and I have to be here." I say and she almost growls at me.

"The dance is next weekend and we still have to go shopping before it." She said grumpily.

"We went shopping last weekend," I try.

"Yeah and?"

I sigh. "Why do we need to go? We already got our dresses when we went with Cam and Brianna."

"We need to get kicked out again!" She exclaims.

I laugh at that. We've gotten kicked out of so many places it's amazing. "How about after the dance we go shopping and go out to eat."

"Deal."

"Hey what's the game plan for the dance?" I ask curiously.

She exaggerates a deep breath, then cuts her exhale short and I laugh once again. "You, Brianna, and I are all going to get ready together. Then, Cameron is going to pick us up at my house and we'll all go to the dance." Ad explains.

"Okay, I've got to go now. Bye idiot," I know she rolled her eyes at that.

"Whatever, later loser." She says before hanging up. Clever.

After ending the call I walk over to my dresser and grab some black shorts and my Slipknot band t-shirt before heading to the bathroom and taking a shower. Once I'm done I step out, get dressed, and then I go into the living room of the basement and lay down on the couch. I turn on the television and flip the channel to Chiller. I watch the movie Priest and slowly drift off to sleep.

The next morning I wake up at six thirty. I stand up and stumble into the bathroom. I took a shower last night but I feel dirty so I take another one. Then, I slip on some ripped black jeans and a white shirt that has black netting as sleeves and says vibes on the front in bold. I apply a little makeup and step into my black and white converse heading out the door for school.

After putting all my stuff away, I travel to the locker rooms for gym. "Great," I murmur. My bag has the word freak spray painted on it in blood red. I pick it up and examine it. There are loud snickers around the room but one girl gives me a look of pity.

"Why does she have to go to school here?" One of the darker complected girls questioned.

"Too many freaks in this world and not enough circuses." Holly said, then a wave of laughter flooded the room. I throw my bag back down onto the floor. I start to walk out when Holly steps in my way. When I try to weave around her our shoulders bump and she backs up a bit."What the hell, I'm standing right here. Are you blind?" she sneers.

"Believe me, looking at a face like that I wish I was." I retort, gesturing to her. That one has been used before but, oh well. The girl that was giving me the look of pity earlier was smiling at me now.

Holly glares at me, which makes no impact. "Bitch," she spat.

"Do you enjoy pointing out the obvious?" I ask, tilting my head. Holly put her hands on my shoulders and slammed me against the lockers. "Ouch, that hurt so much." I say sarcastically. She slapped me across the face and backed up a bit.

When I smile and start to chuckle she gives me a look of bewilderment. "Go to class." She orders the rest of the group that was watching the scene. They all scurry out quickly and then she turns to me again. "Listen closely, freak. Don't try to act all big and bad because you're not. You're nothing and no one wants or likes you. Also, stay away from Graham. You're going to corrupt him. If I see you talk to him again, I'll make you wish you were never born." She tried to threatened me. I already do. "Graham is mine, and if you think he likes you, you're wrong. He calls you the same things we do because that's what you are. He even said that you came on to him once, whore." He did? Well then. She takes one step towards me before finishing. "You're tainted. So stay away from him, you don't want to bring him down with you do you?" I shake my head and she smiles triumphantly. "That's right," she says walking out of the room.

I sigh and walk out as well. I decide not to go to class so I just go to the restroom and lock myself in one of the stalls.

I never came on to him! He lied about me and for that I can't trust him. I still don't want to hurt him but he hurt me. As all these thoughts cross my mind I hear voices coming into the restroom. "I know, I wonder where she went." One of the feminine voices sounded. I sat down on the lid of the toilet and quickly pulled my knees to my chest.

"Holly said that she cried." Another laughed.

"How pathetic." The sound of running water had then filled the room.

"Yeah, what a freak." The second sighed.

"Not only is she a freak but she's a whore." The first said.

"What do you mean, Heather?" The second asked, confused. Then the sound of water ceased.

"Didn't you hear? She tried to sleep with Graham Winters." The one called Heather spoke.

The other, more high pitched voice, had started laughing. "Wow really?"

"Yeah, and Holly said that she threatened her in the locker room." They both laughed.

The voices became distant and the door creaked, which meant that they had left the restroom. I stood up from the toilet and opened the stall door. I went to one of the sinks and turned it on, splashing my face with cool water. When I looked into the mirror I was only disgusted with myself. I didn't come on to him and I'm not a slut. I can't believe he said that.

You can never really trust anyone anymore. They are almost never who they say they are.

I took a deep breath and went to my locker getting all my stuff. I went to the back of the school and went out the door. I'm not staying here. I'm not going to go home either.

I started to walk down into the woods, opposite my house. I walked for about an hour before I finally got to my destination. I was at the rail road tracks. All I could think about was my mom and the time we spent here, before she died.

I step up onto the tracks and begin walking again. I kept going in the same direction, never turning around. Then I started to run and my eyes started to water and then the tears spilled. Eventually, I stopped running. Time must have gotten away from me because it's dark now. I pull my phone out of my bag and check the time. It read 11:41. I had been going for a long time and this is the farthest I have ever gotten into the tracks.

There is a river down over the bank now. The trees are scarce and there are buildings on the other side of the river. I sigh and turn around walking back down the tracks.

When I make it home it's early in the morning, 6:35 to be exact. I step into the shower, then get dressed and head out for school. I haven't gotten any sleep, my legs feel like jelly and my knees are weak. This is great.

Right before my science class I'm walking, more like stumbling, through the halls. I step into the room and set the project on the desk. "Sorry I wasn't here yesterday so I brought it today instead." I explain to the teacher.

She looks down and inspects the work lying before her. "Its fine, your work is extraordinary." She says with a sigh. I smile gratefully and head back to my seat.

Once I get to my seat Graham glares at me. "Relax we got a good grade." I spoke to him lowly.

"Why weren't you here yesterday?" He asks curiously.

"I was for part of it. I left after my second period for the day." I say, not looking at him but down at my notebook.

"Why? And why won't you look at me?" He asked obviously aggravated.

"Doesn't matter. Why are you talking to me?" I asked, changing the topic.

"Am I not allowed to talk to you?"

"Well I don't advise it." I said looking around.

"And why's that?" He asks getting closer. He asks too many questions and he is way to close for my liking.

"Wouldn't want to ruin your image." I retort. What if he gets angry with me and he hits me in front of everyone? Maybe I should tone it down a bit.

"What image?" He questions.

"Your popular." I say softly, and nervously. He's going to hit me.

"Does that mean I can't talk to you?" I can feel his breath on my cheek now.

"You know, you ask a lot of questions." I breathe scooting away from him a little.

"Is that a problem?" I turn to him and give him a tired look which causes him to laugh. I smile a little at that.

"So class, time for the new assignment, Since I gave you yesterday as a freebie. This ones not as fun. You'll be writing a two page-" the teacher said but was cut off by the groans of the students. She rolled her eyes at them and continued. "You'll be writing a two page paper on whatever you choose. As long as it has something to do with science." She added the last part quickly.

"Can it be typed?" One of the students asked.

She sighed and nodded. "Any other questions?" She asked us and when no one raised their hands she turned back to her desk.

"Do you have a computer?" Graham sounded.

"No, I have a laptop." I respond.

"Do you have a printer?"

"Nope." My mom couldn't afford a computer or anything like that. I bought my own laptop and I pay for my own wifi. Although, Jay made me give him the password.

"Okay we can work on it at my house or something," he reasons.

"Okay," I smile weakly at him and he returns it with a strong one.

After that class the rest of day flew by. I hung out with Brianna seeing as Adrienne wasn't at school and Cameron was with Graham somewhere. We were talking and laughing as we walked down the hallway when my knees buckled and I fell. I looked down at my knees and then stood up. Brianna was laughing a little, "Are you okay?" She asked in between giggles.

"Peachy," I replied.

"What happened?" She questioned.

"Oh you know, I walked for a while yesterday and now my legs decided to become flimsy jello. It's great." I replied. The last part was sarcasm.

"Oh," she stifled a giggle.

We continued to walk down the hall as Brianna's name was called out. We turned around and Holly was rushing over to us. "I'm going to go but I'll see you later." I said and she gave me a confused look before nodding.

I went to my locker to get my bag. I have history but I'm not going to do it. The final bell rings and I take my leave.

I open the door to my house and step in. Jay was siting in his chair passed out. At least he's asleep.

As I was about to go into the basement when there was a loud knock at the main door. I looked over at Jay and he stirred, spilling his beer as he rolled over. I rushed over to the door. Who could it be? No one ever comes over. I opened the door to reveal the person and as soon as I see them I'm sent into a panic attack.

CHAPTER 13

"Ms. Fode. Uh can I speak to you?" The deep voice that spoke belonged to Officer Menna.

"Why? Is there a problem?" I question nervously.

"It's about the case. Can I come in?" He asks taking a step closer to me.

"No!" I rush. "I mean we can stay out here and talk." I finish closing the door behind me.

He gave me a confused look. "Okay, well the case, as I said before, has been classified as a hit and run. We can't seem to find who they are though. No one has seen that kind of car anywhere near here. That has led us to believe that it was someone from out of town and maybe even out of state."

"Why don't you just run a scan on their license plate?" I asked shaking my head.

"There was none. We think that maybe the person had removed them before running." He explained. "There were small spots of blood on the ground and trees so we're going to run tests on it but there's no guarantee we'll get a match."

"I know. Anything else?" I ask.

"I have a couple questions for you." He states.

"Okay, question away." I wave my shaky hand around.

"It would be better if we could go inside." He says slowly.

He can't go inside! What am I going to do? "We can't," I mumble.

"Why? What's going on?" he asks narrowing his eyes at me. He's getting suspicious.

"Nothing," I say breathing heavily. I'll just take him down to my room and make sure we're quiet so Jay can't hear us. He's not going to leave and he's getting extremely suspicious, I have no choice.

"I can't help if you don't tell me." He eyes me.

"Follow me," I state. I walk around the house with him in tow and when I reach the doors to my room I open them and let him in.

"Why couldn't we go in the front?" He questioned as I pointed to the couch for him to set. He examines my room before sitting on the couch. I realized that I had left the blanket bunched up at the end of the couch on top of a pillow. He notices too, "Do you sleep down here?" He asked.

What should I say? "Uh, yeah," I nod.

"It's a little cold." He states his gaze remains on me.

"I can turn on the heater." I say, glancing at him.

"It's okay, let's get to the questions." He repositioned himself on the couch to face me as I sat in the chair. "Were you hurt in the accident?"

"Um, not really."

"You got a glass shard stuck in your leg correct?"

"Yes," I scratch the back of my neck.

"Your mom and the child she was carrying passed because of the accident." He clarified, but that was a statement not a question, I nodded. There was a loud bang up stairs causing me to jump and Officer Menna to put his hand on his holster. He walked over to me and put his hand on my back. "We should get out of here."

"Yeah," I said simply, darting for the door. The sooner we're out of here the better. The there was the sound of glass shattering and a groan.

"How do you get upstairs from here?" He asks a little louder than I would've liked. I looked at him pleadingly. He sighed and walked over to the door.

We walked up the hill and down the road. The entire walk was quiet and I kept my head down. Every once in a while Officer Menna would look back at where we had just passed. Once we got into town, we went up to the small diner. He ordered a coffee and I just got a water. "You knew someone was upstairs." he said to me, after smiling gratefully at the old woman who gave him his drink.

"Yeah, I did." I answered honestly.

"Is that why you wouldn't let me in the house?" He interrogated looking up to me but I refused to meet his eyes. After a moment of silence he realized I wasn't going to answer and that was the answer on it's own. "Who was it?"

I can't tell him, It won't end well. "I don't know."

"Reese," he said softly reaching out and putting one of his hands on mine. "I can't help you if you don't tell me what's going on."

"I don't need your help." I snapped immediately. He looked a little startled but then squeezed my hand with a look of pity. Ugh, I hate pity.

"Give me your phone." He demanded, holding his hand out. I looked from his hand to his eyes and back again. "Trust me." I placed my phone in his hand cautiously. He typed something before handing it back to me. I gave him a confused look. "I put my number in your phone. If you ever need anything or you just want to talk, call me." He said sincerely.

I nodded to him. I'm not going to call him, I won't need to. I can take care of myself. We sat in the booth for about an hour just talking. He's actually pretty laid back. I've gotten to know more about him and I don't mind him but I wouldn't say I trusted him.

"Uh, Sir?" An older woman approached us.

"Yes?" He replied.

"We're closing now," She informed us while pointing to the clock on the wall.

"Sorry I lost track of time. We'll leave." He said standing up and paying for the drinks after leaving a tip.

I can't just let him pay for my water."I'll-" I started as we walked into the darkness.

"You're not paying me back." He interrupted, already knowing what was coming. I just stayed quiet and nodded. "I don't want you going home tonight," he blurted randomly.

"I don't have anyplace else to go." I admitted, looking down to my feet.

"You can stay with me." He suggested awkwardly.

"Actually I could stay at my friend Adrienne's," I said. Adrienne's not an option but I know I can't stay with him. I just met him!

"Okay as long as you have someplace to go. I'll drive you there." He agreed as we walked back to my place, where he left his car.

He was very cautious when we arrived at my house and was quick to get me out of there. I showed him Adrienne's house and he let me go. "Thank you for helping me." I said sincerely, scratching the back of my head.

"Anytime," he smiled sweetly showing a small dimple on his right cheek. As I began to walk away he called out my name causing me to turn around. "I've been dancing around this question all night. I don't really know how to ask it and I don't want to make you uncomfortable." He rambled and I stood there waiting for him to actually ask the question. "Are you being abused?"

It's not really abuse, I deserve it. It's my fault that he hits me and many other people have it way worse so I can't complain. I begin to get nervous. How do I respond? I can't tell him that my step dad hits me. I'm pretty sure that even though I don't consider it abuse, a judge will. It could only go down. "N-No," I said stutter."I'm not abused. Why would you think that?" I'm not playing this very cool.

"You have bruises on your arms that look like they could be fingerprints." He noted, staring at my arms. I look down and he was right. You could see the bruises. I thought I had worn a shirt with sleeves long enough to cover them. Obviously not.

I move the sleeve down to cover them and look back up to see his incredibly intense eyes burning into me. "They happened awhile ago. I fell and someone tried to catch me but they grabbed me too hard and it left marks." Nice excuse Reese. Note sarcasm.

He nodded obviously not believing a word I say. "If anyone ever hurts you, call me. Please." The last word was obviously a plead. He really wants to help me, but he can't.

"I will," I lie.

He smiles weakly and drives off. I have a long walk home. So I begin to stroll down the road back to my house. It's chili so I cross my arms. My eye lids become heavy and I'm falling asleep standing up.

When I make it home Jay is definitely not sleeping. Banging and loud smacks echo throughout the house. He comes into view and I stay still, completely frozen in fear. He looks more mad than ever. His eyes lock with mine and I swear I could see fire. He walks hastily up to me and in a stern voice asks, "Where have you been?"

"I-I was with a friend." I stuttered nervously.

"Yeah right, don't lie to me. You know what happens when you do." He sneers, stepping closer.

"I was," I try. Well we're just going to pretend that Officer Menna is my 'friend' for the moment.

Even after already looking enraged he still managed to get even more angry. "That's it." he spat, advancing. He swung his fist at my right rib cage. I didn't hear a crack so that's good. I was having trouble breathing though. He then slammed me up against the door, that was now closed, and did it again. Then he hit my right hip with some small, sharp object. "Go!" He screamed.

And with that I ran to the basement. Closing the door I leaned up against it. I felt a warm liquid running down my hand from where I was holding my hip. I look down to see a cut. It's not too deep so I should be fine. I stumble to the bathroom and clean up the wound, bandaging it.

Tomorrow morning Grandma is coming so I should be safe. I plop down on the couch, and tiredness gets the best of me as I drift off to sleep.

I open my eyes and I have a bit of a headache but I brush it off, walking up stairs. I can hear voices and I step into the kitchen to see Jay and his mom sitting at the counter talking.

My grandma is a heavy woman with gray hair and a faded tattoo of a flower on her ankle. Noticing my arrival, my grandma speaks. "Oh, good morning sweetie."

"Thanks," I reply hugging her.

Looks like Jay cleaned up because everything is a lot more clean than before. "I want to go to the mall today." She announced.

"I'll take yo-" Jay began but grandma interrupts.

"I want Reese to take me." She said, making Jay glare at me. I'm going to hear about this when she leaves. "Let's go." She said expectantly.

"Wait now?" I asked.

"Yes n-" she stopped staring at my shirt. I became confused so I looked down to see the bottom right of my shirt was red from blood. I forgot to change last night. "Honey, what happened?" She asked standing up and hobbling over to me. When she tried to lift my shirt to see the damage I quickly backed up.

"I'll just go change first." I said running to the basement to change. Once I had returned, we left for the mall. "Where do you want to go first?" I asked.

"Let's go to the Starbucks, oh then McDonalds!" She exclaimed. I laughed, at not only her excitement but her wording as well.

This woman never stopped eating! I'm not kidding, she's worse then me! "Okay Grandma, no problem."

We went to all the places she wanted to go to and then some and it was already about eight at night. "Do you want to go to Applebee's?" She questioned.

I chuckled, "Grandma we ate less than two hours ago."

"I'm hungry again." she said simply. I turn to the restaurant and we eat even more. I was completely stuffed.

We were walking around the mall when she suggested we go into Spencer's. After a while she convinces me to go in with her. We left that store and we went to American Eagle. She said she wanted to buy me something for my birthday seeing as she wouldn't be here for it.

Upon walking out I see a group of girls that begin laughing at me and pointing. I already know they're from my school and my being at the mall with my grandma would only add to the insults that were to come. This should be intresting. They approached us and a tall brunette speaks up first. "Reese right?"

I said nothing but the brunette's red headed friend did. "Yeah, that's the girl that stood up to Holly in the locker room." They both looked at me in disgust. "Here with your grandma?" She snickered.

"Well if you're here with your grandma, where's your mommy?" The brunette mocked. Well that hurt.

I don't like to think about my mom a whole lot. "Well if you must know she's a little busy at the moment." I say to them and my grandma looks at me in shock. She knows about my mom but these girls don't. Actually, very few people do.

The girls fake laughed at me. Then again everything about them is fake. The brunette flipped her hair over her shoulder. "Doing what? Is she a whore like you? Let me guess, prostitution."

"Oh come on, I could puke out a better insult than that." I don't want to tell them about my moms death, and I know they were talking about Graham but I chose to ignore it.

My grandma just looked baffled. I don't know if it was because of how the girls were treating me or because of what I was saying but after being silent all this time she finally spoke up. "No, she's underground." I feel hollow now.

"Like, mining?" The red head asked dumbly.

"No, like dead." She said harshly. Well, so much for not telling them.

"Oh, I'm sorry." The red head tried but the brunette just rolled her eyes.

"No you're not. You couldn't care less.You don't care about anything other than yourselves." She said walking off but turned back. "One more thing, don't ever talk to my granddaughter like that again." She warned.

The red head nodded with wide eyes. "See you at school freak." She brunette smirked.

"Wipe that smirk off your face before I rip it off." My grandma snapped at her. Both their eyes widened even more as we walked away.

My grandma huffed as we walked to the car. Once we were in she turned to me. "I'm sorry about th-" I started but she cut me off.

"How long has this been going on?" She said with anger in her eyes.

"What?" I asked even though I already knew.

"I know there are more people that pick on you." She said sternly.

"It's been going on a while," I admitted sheepishly.

"Why didn't they know about your mom?" She questioned, eyes stillstrong even though her voice was wavering.

"I only told a few friends," I said.

Her eyes filled with pity and she slouched in her seat. "I'm sorry, I had no idea."

"It's okay it's not your fault." I murmured softly. She leaned over the seat and hugged me tight. We then took off and headed back home. The ride was loud and normal. I didn't want to go home but she was there so it should be better. Once we arrive, I go to take a shower and then we end up watching a movie.

Grandma's also a thriller lover. My step dad however, is not. So while both Grandma and I watch intensely, Jay is snoring louder than a car alarm. "Jay!" She screams.

"What!" He growls setting up.

"If you're going to be so loud, go to your room!" Grandma demanded. I couldn't help but snicker.

"Mom, I'm forty five you can't send me to my room." He said groggily.

"Wanna bet?" She tested. He groaned and stomped off to his bedroom. Oh how much I love my grandma.

CHAPTER 14

I t's Sunday night and that means it's the last night I'll be able to see my grandma before she leaves. We are eating a normal meal and like always Grandma has her red wine. Let's just say that the dinner is tense.

"Well, you know what your father wanted you to be. Doctors make a lot more money than construction workers." She reminded causing him to roll his eyes.

"Yes, mom but that's not what I wanted to be." He whined, setting his girl down beside his plate.

"I understand but all the construction workers are big doe-doe heads." She said making me laugh. My grandma just said doe-doe heads it's kinda hard not to laugh. Jay glared at me from across the table.

"Not all of them, just your son." I said softly. Grandma busted out laughing but Jay looked enraged.

"That was a good one." She said, taking a drink of her dark wine.

"I'm going to the bathroom." Jay announced, then left.

Grandma stood up to take her plate I the sink. "I'll take it." I told her.

"Oh, thank you. Jay would never have done this." She said, waddling over to the couch.

"No problem." I take the plates to the sink and then come back out to see grandma with her coat on and her purse on her arm.

"Goodbye Jay. I love you, gumdrop." She said pinching his cheeks.

"Yeah I love you too mom." He said, I think that's the first time I've heard him say I love you.

"Bye Reese, I'll see you next time I'm down. Love you." I hugged her. "Oh, and I love your outfit." She noted and then she left. I was wearing a grey tank top with "New York City" written on it in cursive black and a pair of jean shorts. You could still see the fingerprints on my arm but she never noticed.

As soon as the door had closed Jay turned to me with a strong glare. Then, he stomped off to the kitchen.

I knew his mom hadn't treated him the best while she was here but he was really mad. "You disgust me!" he sneered.

"I didn't do anything," I defended.

"You sucked up to my mom the entire time she was here. She treated you like an angel but I was just a piece of gum stuck to her shoe." He began to wash the dishes. Also known as slamming things around and sloshing water everywhere.

"Well you are her gumdrop." I trailed off and he growled. "It's not my fault! She treated you just fine Jay, that's just who she is. She made digs on me to." I said, walking up to the table.

"Not as much as me!" He exclaimed.

"What the hell happened to you?" I questioned harshly. He automatically stopped, completely frozen. He didn't move a muscle.

I mean seriously! His mom is so nice and funny, how'd he happen? I stood quietly by the table, expecting him to start yelling again. However, I was not expecting the damn frying pan to come flying at my face. I quickly put my hands up to block it and with a loud smack and a slight sting I caught it and threw it to the ground.

Then I moved to run out the door to prevent farther damage. I was almost to the basement when his large hands gripped my shoulders and slammed me up against the wall opposite the door. His hands went up to my throat and mine automatically went to his. He squeezed tightly as I thrashed at his hands. My vision was beginning to blur and darkness was closing in. My throat felt as if it was on fire. This is going to be it. Its all over now, I thought to myself. I gave it one last shot and with all my strength a kneed him hard. His face morphed into one of pain as his hands went down to his crotch and he melted to the ground.

I have to get out, I thought. I run into the basement and lock the door behind me. I grabbed the travel bag from behind the couch, still breathing heavily. Once I had packed what was necessary for a couple nights, I fast-walked to the door. I heard a loud bag and stomping. He was coming down the stairs! I quickly slipped out the doors and ran as fast as my legs would carry me. I didn't even know where I was going, just anywhere but here.

So after about three hours of walking around aimlessly I came up to Cameron's house. I hesitantly walked up to the door. What will he think about this? Will he even let me in? I knocked on the door and waited.

Soon he opened the door and once he saw me he looked a little shocked. Then he looked down to my bag. Realization flooded his face as he moved aside for me to come in.

I've stayed at his house before but it's been a while. He's just been distant and I missed him.

"What happened?" He asked once I was inside.

"My step dad and I got in a fight." I said quietly. I was closer with Cameron and Adrienne than anyone else, even my mom.

He took my bag from my hand and started up to his room. "Oh," was all he said... At first. Once we were in his room he turned to me and his eyes locked on my arm. I looked down and saw the hand prints. I forgot about what I was wearing, shit! "What kind of fight?"

I couldn't even look him in the eye. How was I supposed to answer? "He just grabbed ahold of me." I tried to explain.

He walked up to me and pulled me to his bed. "Tell me what happened," he said sternly.

"This happened a couple days ago." I said and he gave me a look. Automatically, I gave in. "I left tonight because I was scared I thought he was going to hurt me really badly," I croaked.

"What happened?" He asked again.

"He threw something at me and then I ran and he caught me a tried to choke me but I kicked him in the nuts. Then, I packed and ended up here." I rushed out, glancing up at him. He just sat there with wide eyes.

"He did what?" Cam growls as his eyes darken.

"You know, maybe I should just go." I say standing up but almost immediately I'm pulled back down.

"You are not going anywhere!" He exclaims. "Knowing you, you'd go back to that hell hole! Sleep there, I'll make a bed on the floor." He said, pointing to the overly large bed.

"The hell you are." I said scooting over, against the wall. He laughed a little as he laid down beside me, covering up the both of us.

"It's been a while since we've done this." He stated, turning to me.

"Yeah, I miss this." I nodded and he looked at me but I couldn't make out his expression.

"Hey...Umm...I have to tell you something," he began awkwardly.

"What is it?" I ask setting up, my face was twisted with confusion and worry. He sits up with me so we are almost the same height. He's still taller than me by about an inch.

"I've wanted to tell you this for a while but I was scared and I was still trying to figure it out and," he rambled on but I interrupted him.

"Cameron just tell me. It's okay," I ensure.

He took a deep breath and closed his eyes. "I'm-" he cut himself short, his eyes still closed.

"Cam, if it's too hard for you to tell me then you don't have to." I said but he shook his head so I waited for him to continue.

"I'm gay," he came out. His eyes shot open to see my reaction. I'm surprised, I didn't think he was. Since he is maybe he would like Mike.

I smile and hug him but he look utterly confused. "I have someone you might like."

"You're not mad or disgusted?" He asked pulling away to look at my smiling face.

"Of course not!" I exclaim.

"I just thought," he started but then his face broke into a smile even wider than mine. "Nevermind, You're the best friend ever!" He said burying his face in my shoulder.

"I'm happy you told me." I said as we settled back into the covers.

"So about this Mike?" He questioned with a smirk. We both laugh and eventually fall asleep.

I open my eyes and roll over. I'm in Cameron's room, but where is Cam? I look up and see the doors open. So I head down to the kitchen. I reach in the cupboard for the cereal and when I turn around Cameron's standing there still in his pajamas.

"I was wondering where you went," he chuckled. He poured his own cereal and we ate. "So I want to talk to you about what happened with Jay." He said looking at me warily.

I sigh, I don't want to! "Cam."

"Reese, you have to talk about it sometime. It's not good to keep it all bottled up. I read it online." He said the last part with a mouthful of cereal and milk.

I breathe a laugh. I know I have to talk about it sometime. I'm just scared but if he could tell me his secret then I should be able to confide in him as well. Right?

"The whole story?" I ask.

"The whole story." He stated.

I sigh and begin, "I was asking for it all night. His mom came to visit and I guess he thought that she was treating me better but she really wasn't. Well I was making mean comments and when his mom left I went in to see what was up with him but he threw something at me and I ran and he tried to choke me but I got away and came here. " I explained.

"Does he hit you often?" He asked.

"Not every night or anything but frequently, yes." I look down to my feet. "He hit mom before the crash."

"How long as this been going on?"

"Ever since I can remember," I shrug

"He stabbed me the other night. I don't know what it was but I didn't do anything about it I just cleaned it up a little." I said look up to see his worried expression.

"You have to go to the hospital." He said sternly.

"I can't afford the bill. I don't need to go anyways it's fine." I brush him off but he pushes farther.

"Let me see it," he demands. I pull my shirt up off my side and rip the bandage off. He gasps at it, I look down. It's all red and irritated. Other than that it's okay. "We are going to the hospital."

"No I'm fine, I just have to clean it again." I tug my shirt back down.

He sighs and then says, "He hits you. You have to go to the cops."

"No!" I exclaim. "I'm sorry but I can't, it won't end well. I'll lose everything and if he doesn't go to jail then the hits will get worse." I panic, tears streaming down my cheeks.

"Oh Reese." he grabs me and hugs me. "He's a monster, I want you to stay with me for a while. At least until Adrienne gets back."

"He mostly hits me when he's drunk so if we just make him cut back in his drinking then-"

"Why are you defending him?" Cam interrupts.

"I just, I don't know." I snuggle back into his chest and just stay there for a while.

We sat there for a little over an hour. Then my phone rang. It said '8 missed calls from Jay The Dickhead'. "Don't answer him or call him back." Cameron says.

I turn and face him. "Thank you Cam."I said sincerely.

"No problem, Reese Monkey." He said ruffling my hair.

"I'm going to go back there." I started and he was quick to object. Shaking his head fast. "Just to get some clothes and some other stuff. Okay?" I asked.

"Alright," he agreed.

I walk home and pack some more stuff before sneaking out the door but before I can get out a voice booms from behind me. "Where the hell did you run off to?"

"I went to a friends." I said quietly.

"You have no friends. Yore the most ugly, fat, and stupid person I've ever met. People like that don't have friends." He yelled in my face. Deja vu!

"Yes, Jay." I look down to the ground.

"Tell me the truth!" He hit the wall beside my head causing me to jump.

"I am!" I yelled back.

"Bullshit! You said that last time and Francis said she saw you with that cop that's working on your moms case!" He shouted.

I stayed quiet. If I spoke I'd only dig myself farther in a grave that I already can't get out of. He punched my rib cage. Now I know there will be a bruise. He slammed my head off the door and threw me to the ground. I stood up and kicked his shin. When he fell over, I grabbed my stuff and ran out of the house.

I saw Cameron's car in my driveway. I should have known he would follow me. I ran to the car and jumped in the back. "What happened in there?" He asked as he sped off.

"He caught me." I reply, placing my bag on the floor.

"What did he do?" He interrogated, his knuckles turned white from his grip in the steering wheel.

"Nothing I got out in time," I lied. He gave me a look that said he didn't believe me so I gave in. "He didn't hurt me bad just punched me a little."

"A little?" He asked, astonished. "You better have your entire closet in there because you're not going back."

"It's okay Cameron." I say and soon he pulls into his drive way.

I take my bag to his room and then we are sat on his couch watching television. "What do you want to watch now?" He asked me, flipping through the options.

"Let's watch The Sacred!" I all but scream.

He jumps a little and puts his hands up in defense. "Jeez woman, you and your scary movies." He said, his eyes wide. Then he smirked, "I was thinking we could watch The Notebook."

"Haha no." I said with fake enthusiasm. He started to smile like a maniac before setting back. "What?"

"You know what I just remembered." he said tilting his head. "It's Monday."

"So?" I asked not understanding what he was getting at.

"So, we skipped school." He informed. We both started laughing. "I can't believe I just now realized that!"

"I wouldn't have realized it at all." I say still chucking a little. "Wait we have school tomorrow."

"Oh yeah okay then I'm going to sleep at eight!" He declared.

"Eight?" I giggled.

"Yeah I have a bed time!" He exclaimed and I busted out laughing again.

"Want a pizza?" I asked.

"Who wouldn't?" He asked in disbelief.

"Touché," I reply, ordering the pizza. We sat there the rest of the day before falling asleep with pizza on our laps.

Chapter 15

The rest of the week had been normal and it's Friday now. Graham has avoided me all week and Brianna just keeps telling me to talk to him.

I open my locker and shove all my books inside heading to science. All I have now is a set of papers. As I walk in the teacher greets me and I take my seat. Graham watches me the whole time.

The dance is tomorrow. I probably won't even go. I know I have a dress and plans with Adrienne and the rest of the group but I'm just not sure anymore. I'll probably just stay in and watch a couple movies. My friends will still have a great time, maybe even better because I'm not there.

"We didn't even work on the assignment." Graham says as soon as I sit down.

"All finished," I responded setting the papers in front of him.

"You did all of it by yourself?" He asked looking through the papers. "This is really good work. I can't take any credit for this."

"You will though. It's fine, it's the last project before the dance. We can work in the next one together." I shrugged and he nodded.

"I'm going to make it up to you," he proclaimed. I nodded to him and looked down to my hands on the table. I could feel his eyes on me but I tried to ignore them. Even when the teacher was talking or when the others were turning in their work. "So, do you have a date for the dance?" He asked trying to be nonchalant. This made me look at him. Can he read minds?

"I was going to go with Brianna, Adrienne, and Cameron." I answered with a tilt of my head.

"What do you mean was?" He questioned.

"Well, I don't know if I'm going to go now." I said and he sat up straight.

"Why not?" He interrogated.

"I don't know, I just don't want to go as much as I did before." I responded as the teacher walked up to us and asked for our assignment.

I handed her the packet and she accepted it with a smile. "This is excellent." She said skimming through the pages. I smiled back at her and she walked over to the next group.

Soon the class ended and I went to math. Before going to study hall I stopped by my locker, packing everything up and then going to class. I got everything so after class I could just leave. Adrienne met me outside of the school.

"Hey," I said walking up to her and getting in Cams car.

"Hey, you ready for a movie night?" She asked as Cameron took off.

"Yeah, are we staying at your house?" I asked her.

"Yes, then in the morning you, Brianna, and I are going to the mall for our hair. Then, we'll go back to my house and do our makeup and get ready." She explained.

"I'll come pick you up after that and we'll all go to the dance." Cameron added looking at me through the rearview-mirror.

"Well I've been thinking about the dance and I just don't know if I really want to go." I said sheepishly.

"You're going." Ad said giving me no choice. I sighed and nodded.

"So where are you staying on Monday?" Cam asked.

"My house," I replied but it was more of a question.

"Do you want to stay at my house?" He questioned.

"Yeah, sounds fun." I agreed with a smile. He looked a little relieved.

At Adrienne's house we all sat around her flatscreen watching the tv show Friends. "So why not just do our hair here?" I asked them and got wide eyed looks from both of them.

"We have to go to the salon for the best results!" Brianna exclaimed.

"Not to mention the not-so surprise spa day I had planned for us." Adrienne informed us, making Brianna squeal. "Facials, manicures, and pedicures." Ad grinned.

"Awesome, I can't wait." I smile at them and continue to watch the show. Shortly after, we fell asleep.

"Get up! We have to get to the mall in time for our spa treatment." Adrienne yelled in my ear. I sat up and got ready.

Eventually, we made it to the mall. "Hey, Twelve o'clock appointment." Ad said to the lady behind the counter.

Her glasses were on the very tip of her nose as she checked the list. "Ah yes, go in that door." She pointed, her blonde hair falling into her eyes.

We went in and sat in a chair. Two ladies came in and took Ad into another room where as Brianna and I got our hair washed. They put some kind of oil in it and wrapped it in a towel. We sat and talked and soon Ad came back out and they took me in. It was a bath. After the bath, I have to admit I smelled pretty good, like vanilla. We went through a massage and a couple other things. Then we were getting our nails done. Mine we're white and black marble with white polkadots on the black strips at the tops.

Brianna's were regular dark blue and Ad's were red with white French tips.

The spa time ended and we went out to eat. We stopped at Applebee's and I had the three cheese chicken penne pasta. Then, went to the hair salon to get our hair styled. When we arrived, the lady immediately took us in. Ad whispered into the ear of my stylist and she smirked before starting on my hair and Ad walked over to her chair.

"Finished," the stylist had said. She spun my chair around and my jaw dropped. My hair was in small curls, all pushed over to the right side of my head as it lays against the front of my shoulder. There was small black flowers along the back that held it over.

Ad came over with spring curls all around her head in a beautiful manner and bump at the top held by to red flower clips. Brianna followed soon after with hair pulled up into an elegant bun with small royal blue flowers. I gave Ad a confused look but she was too busy staring at my hair to notice.

She soon stopped and looked at my face. "We all have flowers in out hair that match our dresses." She said but then added, "You look hot." I gave her a weird look before we paid and left to go back to her house. The next step is makeup. Fun, note my sarcasm.

Soon we were back at her place and they both squealed and dragged me inside and up to Ads room. They pulled out loads of makeup and I looked wide eyed and it. "Wait, wait, wait." I said and they looked at me in confusion. "If you do mine, I do yours." I reason and they nod, continuing to fumble through the makeup and brushes. That's a lot of makeup.

Once they finished, I went to look in the mirror. They appeared behind me, smiling from ear to ear. "You look amazing," Brianna squealed.

"I think beautiful is a better word," Adrienne said. I smiled at myself. I look good. I usually don't but I actually look decent.

"Wow," was all I could say. Ad knew I didn't like my makeup caked. I didn't like foundation either. So she gave me eyeshadow, eyeliner, mascara, and lip gloss. They gave me a brown smokey eye with classic eyeliner, beautiful mascara, and a shiny gloss. Ad has always told me never to match my eye shadow with my outfit. She told me she would disown me if she found out that I had.

"Do you like it?" Brianna asked hopefully. I could only nod as I turn to them. I smile and they jump at me making me flinch on instinct. Then I accepted their hugs.

"Now it's my turn," I smile as they sit down, giving me wary looks. I move to Adrienne first as Brianna plays on her phone. I decide to give her some light blush for her cheeks. Basic white eyeshadow and feline style eyeliner. Another idea struck me. I took a thin brush and put it in silver, sparkly eyeshadow. I draw a thin line right above the eyeliner. I put mascara on her and pulled out the same lip gloss she used on me and applied it to her as well. I examine my work and smile in satisfaction. "Okay, what do you think?" I ask her.

Brianna looks up as well and Ad walks over to the mirror. She gasps and Brianna's jaw drops. "How'd you do this so good?" Ad asked.

"It's just like art, it's easy." I shrugged at her. Brianna sat in the seat and Adrienne smiled at herself in the mirror. "Help me do her make up." I told Ad.

"Okay so what are we going to do?" She asked.

"We could just use grey eyeshadow and the farther we go out the lighter we can go. So from grey to white. We can do wine house style eyeliner and light mascara. Light pink blush to her cheeks and a little lip gloss?" I asked and she nodded

"You do the eyes, I'll do the rest." She said and I gave her a look.

"Thanks, give me all the hard work." I scoff and she laughs as we get started.

We finish and we are all pleased with how we look and our work. We walk down stairs and sit in the couch. I took a deep breath. "We can out our dresses on in like half an hour." Ad said to us as she walked off to her kitchen.

"Are we going to eat?" I asked her and she came back with a bag of chips. "I'll take that as a yes." I said laughing.

We ate some chips and continued to talk. "So Brianna, did you want to go to the dance with someone?" Ad asked her. She immediately blushed.

"Well other than you guys, I was kind of hoping Nick would ask me." She said looking down.

"Oh, do you like him?" Ad asked teasingly.

"No, not yet at least. I just think he's cute." She blushes even more. "Besides I think he likes Holly."

Ad and I burst into laugher and she gives us confused looks. "Are you kidding me?" Ad asks through laughs.

"He doesn't like her. He's attracted to her." I said after sobering up.

"What do you mean?" She asked, clearly puzzled.

"Do you see what she wears? You can see the top of her bra through every shirt she owns. She shows as much cleavage as she can without getting in trouble and her skirts show her butt." Ad points out and Brianna nods in agreement.

"Do you think they've... You know, done it?" Brianna emphasizes the word it. We both give her looks of pity and she bows her head. "I'd figured," She mumbles.

"Sorry but she's slept with almost everyone." Ad informs her.

"I know, when I stayed at her house she was talking about scoring that Brad guy. She also asked a lot about my brother." She said, putting quotation around the word scoring and looking at me when she said the last part.

"I think you're good," I said.

"How am I good?" She asked.

"Graham is currently the only one she wants. She seems to like him more than anyone else anyways. She might stick with him." I assured her and Ad turned to me.

"They aren't dating or anything." Ad had said.

"They haven't hooked up either. Holly would've been gushing about it to everyone if they had." Brianna chimed in.

"Maybe not but it's quite obvious that they like each other." I said looking between the two of them.

"Why didn't you want to go to the dance?" Ad asked.

"I don't know it just didn't seem as exciting anymore." I said, but I don't even believe myself. So how would they?

Maybe the reason I wanted to go in the first place was to have a good time and impress Graham. When I found out what he truly thought of me, I didn't really have as big of a reason to go. I still don't understand why he's so nice to my face. I guess Graham and Holly really are meant for each other. I'm just the freak but for a moment and still right now maybe I...

"Help me get some dip for these chips, Reese." Ads voice snapped me out of my daze. Making me realize that I had been lost in thought for a couple minutes. "Go ahead and keep watching television, we'll be back." She told Brianna, who nodded in response.

Ad pulled the French onion dip out of the fridge. I grabbed a bowl from the cabinet and a spoon from the drawer. When I turned around she was leaning in the table facing me. "What?" I asked.

"You were excited to go to the dance. What really happened?" She asked in sort of a hushed tone.

"It just got really old." I started but Ad interrupted me.

"No, You've been my best friend for as long as I can remember. I think I know when you're lying. Tell me the truth," she demanded.

I sighed. "I really don't know."

She narrowed her eyes at me. Slowly figuring something out that I hadn't even known yet. "Do you think there is a slight possibility you might like Graham?"

I dropped my head, scooping some dip into a bowl and putting the rest in the fridge. "No," I murmured. I walked out of the kitchen and into the living room, setting the dip down on the counter as Ad sat beside me.

I can't help but think about Graham now. I remember the tingles when he wiped the paint off my face. The way he watched me when I was working on the volcano. The compliments that made my stomach flutter. How his hair fell just the right way without even trying. How it felt when I woke up to him holding me. I guess I'm just afraid, but I have to admit it to myself. I like him.

"Yes," I say sadly. I look over to a smiling Adrienne. She wraps me in a hug and I gladly accept it.

"Wait, what am I missing?" Brianna asked, eating another chip. We both laugh.

"Do you want to tell her?" Ad questioned and I nodded.

"I like Graham," I admit. It felt nice to say at first. Then my heart started to hurt.

"Really? That's great!" She exclaimed, eating another chip.

I look over to Ad. "How'd you know?" I asked.

"When you like someone, you try to come up with reasons to convince yourself that they don't like you or that they like some-one else." She points out.

"What? I've only even liked two people including Graham." I said and she smiled.

"I picked up on it." She said and hugged me. "I'm sorry he said those things about you. I'm also sorry you wouldn't let me beat him up."

"Wait what did he say?" Brianna asked.

"You don't know?" I asked and she shook her head.

"He called me a freak and told everyone that I came onto him." I told her and she furrowed her brows.

"That doesn't sound like something he would say and I know my brother," she said. "Are you sure?"

"Not completely." I admitted, you can't trust Holly.

"I'll find out if he really said those things." Brianna assured.

"I don't want to hurt him like I hurt everyone else," I whispered and looked down.

"I'll hurt him before you do." Ad said with a smile, I smile back.

"Let's go get our dresses on." I said and we ran upstairs.

"Don't mess up your hair!" Ad yelled as I slipped on my white and black dress. It was strapless so I just pulled it up from the bottom.

"Are you girls ready yet?" I heard Cam shout from downstairs.

"Almost," Brianna hollers back. I can just imagine him groaning. We touch up our makeup and head down stairs.

Cameron gawks at us and I hug him when I see him. He soon snaps out if it and looks at me again. "Okay, let's go." He ushers us out the door.

"I can't wait," Brianna squeals when we hop in to Cams car.

CHAPTER 16

The whole way there all I heard was squeals coming from the back seat. "Do you think I look good enough?" I heard Brianna ask. I rest my head against the window. Being in cars have made me a bit tense ever since what happened with my mom. "We're here," Cam said as he shoved the door open and nearly fell out of the car. Must have been the squeals.

I see him walk around to my door and open it for me. He held his hand out for me to take and I did as I stepped out of his car. What a gentleman. He did the same for the girls and laced his arm with mine. "Ready?" I asked. He hummed a reply as we walk up to the doors. The girls were already in there, of course.

I notice a group of guys leaning against the building. Probably avoiding going in before they have to. The girls are going to be clingy so I guess it would be good to have a moment to relax. We walk in and there was already a bunch of people here. I walk up to the girls and they are already by the punch table.

"I want to get some punch before it's spiked." Ad says as she takes a drink and then starts to cough. "Too late."

"I'm going to go see my brother, I'll be back." Brianna announces as she walks off in a random direction. The music that was playing now was upbeat. People were jumping around everywhere. Then the music slowed down and people paired up into two. Except this group of guys that were huddled in a circle, wasted already.

"Let's dance," Cam suggested and I looked up at him. He was smiling down at me.

"I can't dance!" I said and shook my head violently. I've never even tried.

"I'll show you, it's easy." He said pulling me out onto the dance floor. He rested his hands on my hips and I put mine on his shoulders. "Now just sway your hips and move with me." He explained, leading me through the song. This was the first time I've ever danced with a guy, or danced at all.

As the song went on, I picked up the moves and didn't need help. Cam whispered something but I could barely hear him. "I can see the bruises on your arms." As soon as I made out what he said I began to panic. I forgot about them. Looking at my arms to see for myself, very faint bruises marked my arms. You could only tell if you were looking right at them.

"They are almost gone, no one will notice." I tried to convince both him and myself. "Especially in this light," I added. He shook his head at me.

"So you're still staying at my place on Monday right?" He asked and I nodded.

"I just need to pack up some stuff to stay." I told him and he looked a little uneasy. "What?" I asked.

"I just don't want you going there." He admitted to me. I gave him a look.

"I'll be fine, Cam. I've stayed there most of the week and I haven't even seen him. Besides, I think he's calmed down by now." I said sincerely.

"You stayed there all week?" He asked in bewilderment, almost yelling. I flinched back a little at that. "I'm sorry. I didn't mean to scare you." Cam said and I hugged him.

"You didn't, you just surprised me." I assured and he relaxed a bit.

"You say he's calmed down but he almost killed you, Reese. Anger like that can be sparked easily with people who have issues. I just don't want you getting hurt. I'll feel better knowing your staying with other people this weekend." He said and I furrowed my eyebrows. He seemed to notice my confusion. "You're staying with Brianna and Adrienne tonight right?"

"No, I'm going home." Right after the words left my mouth I regretted it. He tensed up almost immediately. "I'm staying with you on Monday though."

"You'll be there all night and all day Sunday. You're bound to run into him." He said, not even looking at me.

"If I stay downstairs I'll be fine." I declared.

He looked at me with a small glare. "If he hurts you ever again, I'll kill him." He sounded very sure of himself. All I could do was nod and hug him. He hugged me back tightly.

The song ended and he pulled me off the dance floor to got some punch. We walked over and Brianna was standing next to Ad, talking to Nick. She's talking to him with a very large smile and he was smiling back. Ad was giggling and pouring herself some punch. I'm not so sure what it is now.

I walked behind Nick to get to the other side of the table. On the way I gave Brianna a knowing look and she blushed. I poured myself some punch and joined Ad in her giggling. "What are you guys giggling about?" Nick asked curiously.

"Nothing," Ad replied with a smile and I tried my hardest not to laugh.

"This is just really good punch." I lied, Brianna's face was about almost the shade of fire as she fiddled with her bracelet.

"Okay?" He said but it was more if a question. "So Brianna, do you wanna dance with me?" He asked in a shy manner. I've never really known Nick, I've never even talked to him until now but he was always sort of outgoing and flamboyant from what I saw of him. He was never shy. Looks like someone might like Brianna. I smirked at that thought.

She nodded to him and he grabbed her hand, which only made her blush more, her face was about as red as a fire truck when he lead her to the dance floor. I looked over to the corner of the room by the door and I saw Graham. He looked very handsome. He was wearing a formal black suit with a black tie and a white cloth sticking out of the pocket. His hair was styled in his messy do as usual and he had a clear cup in his hand. He was watching Nick dance with his sister.

Holly skipped over to him and grabbed him by the neck. She was wearing a low cut peach dress that barely covered her bottom. Not like the guys cared, they couldn't keep their eyes off of her. She kissed him roughly, surprising him. She then said something to him and pulled him out to the dance floor. Ouch, that hurt but it's not like he likes me and I don't own him. He likes Holly and he thinks I'm a freak, that's why he said those things about me. I just look away from the sight as quick as I can but Ad caught me before I could. She followed my line of view and then gave me a look of pity. Holly was now kissing Graham's neck. I rolled my eyes and took a drink.

"Don't look at me like that," I deadpanned. She just continued to do it as she laughed a little. "I'm going to the restroom, I'll be right back." She nodded and I walked off.

When I got to the restroom, I looked in the mirror. My make up was still intact. Maybe he'll notice me? No stop it! He doesn't like you! I need to get over this crush thing, it's ridiculous. The drink from earlier gave my mouth a weird taste so I washed my mouth out before pulling my dress back up a little and walking back to Ad. She was smiling triumphantly.

"You look creepy." I noted and she just smiled more. "Your face is going to break or something, stop!" I yelled horrified.

"Everything is working out. It's going to be a great night!" She exclaimed. Yeah, my nights going great. Notice my sarcasm.

I looked around and everyone was either sitting down or standing along the dance floor but no one was in it or dancing. There was no music either. "What's going on?" I asked.

"Some drunk kid spilled the so called punch on the Dj's equipment. They are cleaning it up in hopes it's not ruined." Ad informed me. I lauded a little at that. The music started back up and it was another upbeat song.

I looked over to the sitting area and I see Brianna almost on Nicks lap kissing him, and he's definitely enjoying it as much as she is. I slapped Ads arm and she glared at me for a moment before I pointed over to them with my jaw dropped. Soon her's dropped too and then we smirked and laughed.

"So what were you smiling so wildly about?" I questioned and she smiled again.

"I told you, this will be a good night." She responded vaguely. I gave her a look and she sighed before continuing. "Brianna and Nick were dancing and having a good time."

"Yes, they are cute together." I said with a smile. I bet they will end up dating.

"After you left, Holly kept kissing on Graham." She said and I raised my eyebrow at her.

"Thanks for that information," I mumbled and grabbed my half empty glass taking a sip.

"You didn't let me finish," she whined. I looked at her and waited for her to continue. "Well, he pushed her off him and she tried to go after him but he shrugged her off again. He gave her a very mean look before she turned and walked back to her friends, almost in tears. After that he just left," She explained. I couldn't help the tug of my lips into a small smile. I know it's wrong but I couldn't help it.

Ad noticed and she laughed at me. "That's sad," I said but it was obvious by the slight smile that I wasn't sad at all. She knew too which made her laugh even harder.

"Come on, let's dance." She suggested as another upbeat song came on. Honestly, I don't know any of the songs. I don't listen to this type of music. There seems to be a lot of it though. We dance and dance, even to the slow songs like the idiots we are, until she starts to complain about her feet hurting. Then we sit down. This night might not suck after all.

I feel a vibration on my side. I pull my phone out and see its a missed call from Jay. Along with thirteen others and two text messages. Spoke too soon. The messages read: Where are you? I've searched the entire house and you're not here!-J

He hasn't learned how to shorten his words and using numbers was out of the question. The second message read: I've called you eleven times and you still haven't answered. Where are you? We need to talk, now!-J

Just as I finished reading that message I received another: Fourteen missed calls now, if you are trying to test my patience it won't end well for you. I will make you pay and it will hurt! Do you want more scars?-J

The last message made my skin crawl and it honestly scared me. I hated my scars but I deserve them. I deserve everything I get, otherwise he wouldn't do it. He loves me because if he didn't then he wouldn't be adopting me. I need to learn discipline and I need to learn not to talk back. I deserve it, I deserve everything.

I don't want him getting mad so I should call him back. "I'll be back. I need to make a call." I told Ad and she smiled.

"We'll continue our dancing when you return." She announced with a slight slur. I shook my head and smiled to her before walking off. As soon as the cool breeze hits my skin I get goosebumps. I can see my breath so I know its quite cold. I feel as if someone is watching me but I quickly brush off the feeling as I dial his number.

It only rings twice before he picks up. "Where are you?" he asked immediately.

I sigh, "I'm at the school dance."

"Why didn't you answer me when I called and texted?" He asked persistently.

"I don't have any service in there and I was busy." I ground out. I was getting annoyed with all his questions. I do, however, have to admit that he seems a lot calmer than usual. He's not as mean.

"You could have told me you were going. You are aware you have to be punished, right?" He questioned and I gritted my teeth.

"Yes," I hissed. I heard footsteps behind me but I just thought it was a random person so I didn't bother turning around. Instead I just lowered my voice.

"I could knock you out in a second and you wouldn't remember anything when you woke up so don't talk to me like that! Do I need to get the knife?" He threatened. I flinched at the loudness of his voice. I think anyone within ten feet of me could've heard that. I sighed replying a simple no. "Good, now I want you home before midnight. I have new information about your mother and your little cop friend. Don't make me have to come after you." And with that he hung up. I huffed out a breath as tears stung my eyes the cold made my arms and legs numb.

"Who was that?" I familiar voice sounded. I turned around to see Graham in all his glory looking right at me. He had his hands tucked inside his pockets.

"Nobody you know," I wasn't lying he didn't know Jay. He smiled a bit causing me to smile too, just a little.

"Can I ask you a question?" He asked me. I had been avoiding him for a while.

"You just did," I joked and he laughed slightly. It looked like something was bothering him. "What is it?" I asked, tilting my head.

"Why are you giving me the cold shoulder?" He asked and my smile fell.

"All of me is cold, it's practically thirty degrees out here." I exclaimed and he walked up to me giving me a look. I sighed and answered his question. "Someone told me the things you said. I know what you truly think about me. I know you think I'm a freak and I know you lied about me. You said I came on to you, I just haven't figured out why." I said and he looked taken back.

"I would never say anything like that about you." He said and I almost believed him, almost.

"It's okay I understand. Everyone else feels like that too but why did you have to lie?" I asked and he shook his head.

He took his hands out of his pockets and grabbed my arms gently and a little above my bruises. As soon as he touched me I felt tingles up and down my arms. His warm touch was soothing. "I would never say anything bad about you or anything that would upset you. I never want to hurt you and I would never lie about you, ever! That includes calling you a freak because I don't believe you are. I think you are amazing and unique and beautiful. I promise you I never said any of that." He stared right into my eyes as he said that. The intensity in his stare and the sincerity behind his words made me truly believe him. I was blushing insanely as well. I felt bad about accusing him of something he didn't do.

"I'm sorry," I apologized, looking down. He put a finger under my chin to make me look at him. When I did he shook his head at me again.

"Don't be sorry. Who told you all of that?" He asked and then I just felt foolish.

"Holly," I muttered. He studied my face after I said it, smiling slightly but trying to hide it.

"Don't listen to anything she says, okay?" He asked and I nodded. Then he pulled me into a hug. My breath hitched and he held me lightly, stroking my hair.

"You're going to be in trouble if you mess up my hair. Adrienne will be after you," I laughed against his chest as he chuckled.

"You're sort of cold, let's go inside." He said wrapping his arm around my shoulder and holding me close. I'm not tense when he does it now, I don't think he'd hurt me. We walked in and Adrienne was dancing with some guy. Brianna was just talking with Nick and Cameron was with a group of guys around the punch. A slow song then came on and I heard Graham mumble the words perfect timing. "Dance with me?" He asked, scratching the back of his neck and blushing slightly. I smiled and nodded to him. I placed my hand in his as we walked out to the dance floor. He placed his hands on my hips, holding me a lot closer than Cameron had. I wrapped mine around his neck as we swayed. I was immediately comfortable with him. I may not be the best dancer but I didn't care at the moment.

Graham rested his forehead against mine and closed his eyes. I kept mine open for a little while longer. He was smiling widely, like he'd just won a medal or something. I closed my eyes then and he held me even closer. My chest was now against his from how close we were but for once, I was comfortable with it. Maybe even liked it.

CHAPTER 17

(Graham's POV)

As I dance with Reese, I can't help but think of those things Holly told her. No doubt they are lies, I would never do that to Reese. I really like her and I'm still surprised she had believed them in the first place.

I wonder why Holly would say those things. Was it to get back at me for something? To get Reese to stay away from me? I don't know, but I'm going to find out.

It angered me to see how hurt she was. There was also that other feeling, when she thought I said those thing she was hurt. Which means she finally let me in, behind all those walls she had built up to protect herself from everyone. I was mad that Holly had done that but I was happy to know Reese had let me in. I'm twisted, I guess.

It really hurt me when she wouldn't talk to me over the week. I kept wondering what I did and thought she needed her space so I let her be. Maybe that's why she was mad, because of Holly. I was going to ask her to the dance but she said she wasn't going. Plus, I thought it wouldn't be a good idea considering she was mad at me.

That night Holly called me and asked what my plans were. I told her I was going with friends and she told me I wasn't. She said I was going to go with her and apparently I had no say. It made me a little mad but I just let her do her thing. It's not like I was planing on spending the whole evening with her. The only reason I wanted to go was because Brianna told me Reese was going.

It actually scares me how much I like her. I never thought I would and Nick warned me about her. I just couldn't stay away. When I touch her, as girly as it sounds, I felt good and I got this tingly feeling throughout my body. She always tensed up though. Which confused me. I have yet to figure out about all that.

I started to like Reese almost two weeks ago. I spent most of my time trying to convince myself that I didn't but it was no use. I like her and I'll freely admit that to anyone, except Reese. Just for now, I will tell her when I feel I can without anything going wrong like Holly interfering. I don't know what Reese's reaction will be but I hope it's good.

Right now is the most happy I've been in a while. I'm so happy to have her in my arms. She's not the slightest bit tense. She doesn't seem to get tense at all anymore. I pull her closer to me, our chests were touching as we swayed. I open my eyes for a second and she had hers closed, so I closed mine again and continued to think.

I'm going to spend more time with her. I'm going to make her happy. I'm going to be there for her when ever she needs me. Not everything about her was perfect, but no one is. She's perfect for me. Hold on, did you really just think that?

At least I didn't say it out loud. I hope I didn't. Nope, I'm good.

I wonder who she was talking to on the phone? It was a guy and he was absolutely angry from the way he yelled. I didn't hear what he said though. That's one of the few things that bother me about Reese. I want to know who she was talking to and why he was so angry. I know it's none of my business but I worry about her. I want her safe.

I also want to know why she's so secretive and what she's hiding. I know it's connected to why she always flinches away from people. Sudden movements and loud noises put her on edge and she flinches at those too. She's almost always tense as well. Maybe something tragic happened before I met her. I would say it was what happened with her mom but she was like that before. I only recently found out the whole story.

Her mother was pregnant and both her and the baby had died on impact but it was a hit and run. They are slowly figuring stuff out but it takes a lot of time. It must be killing Reese inside to have to wait for her mothers justice. Bad choice of words.

The music had stopped and I opened my eyes to see those big hazel ones looking right back at me. They were filled with so much emotion, it was amazing. I pulled my head from hers and smiled. She smiled back and tugged me over to the punch bowl. It's safe to say there is no longer any punch in there. Adrienne was over there smirking at both of us. Cameron was watching me warily and Brianna was looking at Reese with a big smile. Nick right behind her giving me a small smile. Maybe he knows he was wrong about her?

She tried to reach for a drink Adrienne was handing her but she dropped it before Reese could grab it. Making every one back up. Including Reese, who backed up right into me. "I'm sorry, I'll get some paper towels." Adrienne muttered before walking off.

Reese followed her and they came back with loads of paper towels to help clean it up. "Sorry about your shoes," Reese said looking guilty. She didn't even do anything.

"They were old anyways," I shrugged off. They weren't though. They belonged to Holly's father. She made me wear them and now they aren't new anymore. Sorry Mr. Cherish, at least the rest of the suit is mine.

Reese smiled at me and I brought her closer. She stumbled a little but I kept ahold of her. I wrapped my arms around her back and squeezed. I let go because it would have been weird to hold her all night. She moved away to go with her friends to the bathroom or something.

Cameron walked up beside me. "You better not hurt her." He said loud enough for only me to hear. I looked at him for a moment in shock.

"What?" I asked dumbly. I knew what he was talking about, Reese. He was afraid I was messing with her.

"Don't hurt her. She's been hurt enough." He said angrily, looking down to his feet as if remembering something. Maybe a past boyfriend had hurt her but I won't.

"I would never to that to her." I feel like I've said that a lot tonight.

"Do you like her?" He asked bluntly.

"Yes," I admitted and he looked up.

"When you find out about her secret, you can't lash out." He said to me. I knew she had a secret! Could it be that bad? As if reading my mind he said, "Yes it is, but it's not her fault."

"When will she trust me enough to tell me?" I asked curiously.

"She won't," he said and I looked down. Wow, thanks dude that was a real confidence booster. "She didn't even tell me until she was forced too and she still hasn't told either of the girls. You will have to find out yourself. You will though it's impossible to miss, you'll find out and you'll only want to do one thing."

"What's that?" I question.

"I can't say. Trust me it sucks to know. Especially, when you can't do anything about it." He said looking down then back up at me. Suddenly realizing he's said to much he cleared his throat. "It's obvious she likes you too. Keep in mind that if you hurt her, I'll hurt you."

My mind was exploding with all this unfinished information. The thought of her liking me back was enough to put a smile on my face. Cameron and I were cool now but he would hurt me if I was to hurt Reese. I won't so I don't have to worry about that. Then there was that nagging feeling I had. I want to know what her secret is so bad. I just wish she'd tell me but as Cameron said I'll know soon enough. I'll just have to be patient.

The girls returned and I finally got a good look at what Reese looked like in good lighting. The light in the hallway was on so I saw everything perfectly clear. I knew she was beautiful but wow. Her makeup was done well but the colors of the eyeshadow are what made her eyes pop. Her hair was done very nice. The white dress with black vines came mid-thigh on her. It was actually elegant, unlike half the people here. I looked her up and down, trying not to be a pervert, I just thought she was beautiful. She walked up to me and I swallowed hard.

"Reese! Let's dance," Brianna yelled to her and she turned back to me giving me a small smile before being dragged away by my sister and their friend. I watched as she danced. You sound like a stalker. I knew I did but she just moved like no one was watching. Honestly, I was probably the only one. I'd just never seen her like this or at least to this extant.

She moved to the beat until it was cut off. The group of them walked over to the seating area and everyone who didn't have a seat stood by as the principle walked up on stage. "I think that this game was a major success. Id like to congratulate all the players on their win and I know you guys will do great in the future. You worked as a team and that's what got you through it. Now I will announce the homecoming queen and king." The principle spoke loudly.

I just stood there as I wait for her name to be called. I knew Holly would win. She's popular so it's a given.

"The homecoming queen is, Holly Cherish!" He said and she acted surprised. Why? I have no idea. She knew as well as I did that she was going to win. "Joining her in stage will be her king. Nick Sanches!" Poor Nick. I know he has a thing for my sister but if he hurts her I'll- Wait, that's how Cameron feels about Reese! Like she's his sister, I know how he feels now.

After announcing the dance between the king and queen, the principle bids us farewell as he leaves the stage. Nick is holding Holly as far away as possible as they dance to some song Holly picked. I could see him sending looked of distress towards my sister who just giggled at him. When their dance was over everyone was allowed to dance again as they played a fast song. Everyone was dancing, even Cameron. I was just leaning on the wall.

Some drunk guy was dancing with Reese. Harmless right? Except the fact that he was all over her! His body was pressed up against hers. Granted that's how everyone was dancing but it still bothered me. Once he started to let his hands roam a little, it took a lot to not walk over there and knock him out. She gently pushed him off her and he got the hint and walked away. She continued to dance with her friends though. Reese glanced up, saw me, and frowned. She walked over to me once again making me swallow hard.

"What's wrong?" She asked tilting her head ever so slightly to the left. It was just so cute.

I smiled down at her, "Nothing." I'm lying, I think I might have been a little jealous.

She smiled lightly and grabbed my hand. She started pulling me out to the dance floor but I planted my feet firmly. "Come on, just have some fun."

"I was having fun. Watching you and some drunk guy dance the night away." I replied bitterly and she looked a little hurt so I caved in. "I'm sorry," I sighed.

She smiled a little like she'd just realized something and she took my hand and squeezed. "Please come dance?" She asked and I couldn't say no to something so stupid so I let her pull me over with a wide grin. She started to dance again and I did the same.

It was fun, until my feet started to hurt. I sat down beside Reese and nudged her a little. "Having fun?" I asked and she smiled and nodded. "Well I don't know about you, but my feet hurt." That made her laugh. I couldn't keep my eyes off her, except when I closed them. There she was though, right there in my head as well.

After a while a slow song came on. I held my hand out to her as if asking to dance and she took it standing up. I lead her out to the dance floor and once again placed my hands on her hips. She smiled as I pulled her closer. So close to where her petite figure was pressed hard against my larger one. She laid her head on my chest and I rested my chin on her head. We swayed comfortably until I heard a scream. It wasn't a scared scream it was an angry one and it came from Holly.

She marched over and slapped me across the face. It didn't even hurt. She was trying to make a scene and she was going to get one. She got whatever she wanted. If she wants this than so be it.

Reese stepped away from me quickly with a confused expression. "How could you?" Holly screamed. "How could you cheat on me with her?" She said that word with so much disgust that I have to grit my teeth so I don't snap. Reese's face morphed to one of hurt and I instantly wanted to change it.

"Don't ever talk about her like that again and you are not my girlfriend." I narrow my eyes at her.

"It doesn't matter, you came here with me. Now let's go." She reached for me but I back away. "What's your problem?"

"You're my problem. I was dancing with Reese and you just slapped me. I'd much rather spend my night with her than you." I say walking over to Reese.

"Baby, you don't mean that." She said but I shook my head, feeling the need to throw up when she called me that.

"Yes I do," I reply. She looks enraged as she approaches Reese and I.

"You did this, bitch!" With that she shoved Reese to the ground. When Reese landed in her hip she let out a cry. She put her hand over it and held it tight but she didn't get up. I dropped to her side and touched her head. Her face was clearly showing pain. It couldn't have hurt that much, she did hit the ground hard though.

Anger swirled within me. I help Reese up and she looked fine. She glared at Holly. "What the hell?" She exclaimed. A crowd grew around us.

"You deserved it. I didn't even push you that hard, you're faking it." Holly accused. Reese looked like she was having an inner battle. She looked like she was debating something.

"It hurt a little more than you would think." She murmured, but I heard it. Holly must have to because she rolled her eyes.

"You stole him from me." She snarled. "Remember those things he said about you. You're a freak and no one wants you. What makes him any different?" She whispered to her.

Reese smiled bitterly and I took that as my cue to say something. "What exactly did I say?" I asked her.

"You...umm...y-you... It doesn't matter." She stuttered. Now my anger was at it's peak. I glanced up to see Cameron making his way towards us. He looks more angry than me as he stopped right in front of Holly.

"Shut the hell up, you stupid bitch," he shouted. "You don't know what she's been through. Her mom died-" he stopped turning to look at her. She was looking at him with absolute adoration. Also giving him a wary look. As if to keep him from saying something or to stop him in general. He turned back, "Leave her alone. She shouldn't have to deal with half the shit she does! So lay off!"

He walks over to Reese and his eyes narrow at her side. I follow his gaze and see a red stain. She's bleeding. I rush to her side to check out the damage. "What happened?" I asked.

"I bet I already know," Cameron says bitterly. Reese looks down and nods. His jaw clenches and I want to know what they are talking about.

"It was last week." She tries but it doesn't work.

"It wouldn't have started bleeding again. It's more fresh than that. When did he do it and do not lie to me." He said. He? Who's he? I swear whoever touched her I will-

"Sunday," Reese interrupted my thoughts. He shakes his head and pulls her into a hug. "Thank you," she said to both of us.

"I think the parties over now." Cameron says as everyone begins to leave.

"Let me walk you home." I offer Reese, who smiles and nods.

"I don't like this," Cameron whispers to her and she just hugs him whispering something in return that I didn't catch.

I walk her home and it's silent the whole time. We reach her front porch and I begin to wonder why she never let me come in up here. "Thank you for everything. I really appreciate it." She rushes a little. Her eyes were swirling with all kinds of emotion. She leaned forward and kissed me on the cheek. My eyes widen in shock and bliss. She smiles a little at my huge grin and darts inside.

At home I open the door and my father is siting at the table. A beer in hand and he's mumbling to himself. "Where's mom?" I ask and his head shoots up.

"She's asleep." He murmurs to me. I nod to him. His eyes were red and puffy so he's been crying. Did they fight?

"What's wrong?" I ask.

He looks straight into my eyes. "I've messed up, son." He stalked off to the bedroom and I stayed there. Sitting completely confused.

CHAPTER 18

(Reese's POV)

I just kissed him on the cheek! What was I thinking? I'm so stupid! I watched as he walked away. I looked at the clock and it said it was one. Shit I'm late!

"Where have you been?" Jays voice was low behind me. I spun around and faced him. He was a lot closer than I thought. He grabbed my hips and slammed me against the door. That I just had shut.

"I had to walk. I didn't have a ride. So I'm a little late." I rushed to explain but he didn't want my excuse. He punched me in the jaw right where the other bruise was.

"We need to talk." He growled at me. Gripping my arm as hard as he could, he jerked me to the couch. "What are you doing with that cop?"

"He wanted to know about the crash so he asked a couple of questions." At first. It was the truth, just not the whole truth.

"Okay," he trailed off. Calming down a little. "What about that boy you were with outside?"

"He's just a friend." I replied but his anger had risen again. He slammed his fist on the table causing me to jump.

"A friend that you were sucking face with?" He asked harshly.

"I only kissed him on the cheek!" I defended myself which angered him more. He threw his fist and it connected with my eye. I pushed myself away from him and stumbled to the other side of the room. He followed me and grabbed my throat. With his other hand he pushed his hand on my side.

I scream out in pain from the slice that had re-opened earlier when Holly pushed me. "It's bleeding again is it? Maybe you should tell your boyfriend about it. Oh, or your cop friend." He snarled and threw me to the floor. Grabbing my hair he dragged me up the stairs. He shoved me into the closet and locked the door. "I'll let you out when you learn a lesson."

What lesson was I supposed to learn? I started to cry as I beat on the door. I begged and pleaded for him to let me out. I beat on the door until my knuckles turned bloody. Eventually, I fell asleep. Then I woke up and it seemed like months I was in there.

Suddenly, the door opened and Jay picked me up. "Have you learned your lesson?" He asked holding me by my hair again.

"Yes, sir I'm sorry." I apologized quickly. He gave me a disgusted look and the next thing I knew I was tumbling down the stairs. I hit the bottom and smacked my head off the banister. "Please stop," I cried.

I could taste blood. My lip was split. I tried to pick myself up but I was too weak. He came to the bottom of the stairs and hovered over me. Then, he just walked away. I mustered up all my strength and took myself to the couch. He sat beside me with a knife in his hand. "You're pathetic, at least your fat ass lost some weight. Maybe I should lock you in a closet with no food again. You didn't even make a sound for two days. I was impressed," he said.

"Two days?" I exclaimed. He covers my mouth with his hand.

"Shut up!" He snaps and I whimper. Looking down at my hands and keeping my mouth shut. I don't want to get hit anymore. "You are disgusting. Luckily I won't have to live with you for long." He mumbles to himself. He's right I'll be done with school in a year and then I'll be gone, finally.

I'm slowly becoming lightheaded. He tosses the knife into my hands. "What?" I asked him confused.

"Cut," He demands. I look at him horrified. "Do it!"

"No!" I all but yell. He's face is so close to mine I can see the little stubble on his cheeks.

"I said do it. You're pathetic anyways. No one wants you and no one cares about you. You'd only be making peoples lives easier." He tells me, causing my eyes to tear up.

I bring the knife up to my wrist and press but not hard enough to cut. So many things run through my head. How much Cameron cars about me. Everything Adrienne and Brianna have done for me. The words that Graham's had said to me. I think you are amazing and unique and beautiful. I smile at the thought. I'm stronger than this. "No, I won't do it."

"How dare you defy me?" He yelled. "You're mother was killed and she left me in charge of you! You're my step daughter and you will do as I say!"

Didn't he have something to tell me about my mom? I guess I'll have to find out myself. I threw the knife at his face. Which resulted in cutting the bridge of his nose. He yelled as I ran out of the house. I ran all the way to Cameron's house. I knocked on the door. I had no idea what time it was but less that thirty seconds after I knocked he opened the door with wide eyes.

"I will kill him!" He exclaims and tears stream down my face. He's eyes soften and he pulls me to him. He carrys me upstairs and to his bed. Lying down with me he just hold me as I cry. I glance at the clock beside his bed and it says; 12:07. I can't sleep so I lay with my head on his chest. "We need to clean you up," he whispers in my ear.

I nod to him and he lifts me up, carrying me to the bathroom. He sets me on the sink and finds alcohol bottles. "I usually attend to these myself." I say and he sighs.

"You shouldn't have to," he mumbles. "I need to make a call, I'll be back." He announces walking off. He comes back in five minutes with his cellphone in hand. "I called Graham."

"What why?" My eye widens. The other eye was swollen so only one was fully functional.

"You should tell him. He likes you and he deserves to know what he's getting himself into." He reasons and he's right.

"Yeah, I guess you're right. Just now is not the time. I will tell him though, I promise." I told Cameron and he smiled slightly at my compromise.

"Okay," he says and we hear a door slam. "I think he's here." He laughs a little.

"Where are you guys?" Graham yells from down stairs.

"In the bathroom," Cameron yells back. Soon he was in the doorway. Cameron was cleaning up my lip when he walked in. He was at my side in a second.

"Are you okay? What happened?" He held my face in his hands.

"I just got in a fight with some guy on the street," I lied. I hate lying, especially to him.

"What did he look like?" He was fuming.

"It doesn't matter." I tried but he shook his head, looking at me in bewilderment.

"It matters to me, please?" He asked. I'm so confused! I want to tell him but I can't yet. I want to so bad.

"I don't remember," I croaked out. It pains me to do this. I can't take it. My eyes glass over and I threw myself at him. Wrapping my arms around his neck, sniffling into his chest. He grabbed ahold of me and held me close but not too tight.

"Let's get you cleaned up." He said pulling away from me. He grabbed the bottle of alcohol and purse it over my knuckles. I hissed as it stung. He looked up and mumbled an apology. I can see Cameron smirking from the corner of my eye. I rolled my eyes at him as Graham moved up to my face. He gets a paper towel and pours the alcohol onto it. He cleans my eye and then goes down to my nose. After that he stops at my lip. He's eyes flick up to mine and then back down to my lip. He very slowly wiped it off. He folded the paper towel and started cleaning into the cut. I hissed and grabbed his hand. He was looking frantically between my lips, hand, and eyes. He gulped and his face got a little closer. My breath hitched.

Is he gunna kiss me? I want him to kiss me. I hope he kisses me! Wait, I can't let him kiss me until he knows the truth. If he doesn't want me then that's okay but he needs to know before he kisses me. I close my eyes and sigh then pull away from him. "I'm sorry, but you have to know something first." I explained.

"Okay what is it?" He asked still very close. He looked so cute when he was confused.

"I-I can't tell you yet," I sighed again and he just put his head on my shoulder.

"Really?" I hear Cameron yell. "So close," he mumbled as he stalked off.

"Tell me when you're ready," he says and then hesitantly kisses my cheek causing me to blush. He finished cleaning me up and then helped me off the sink.

"You're not going home," Cameron says as soon as my feet hit the carpet of his room.

"Where am I staying tonight then?" I ask and he smiles.

"With me!" He exclaims. I laugh at him and mumble an okay. "I don't want you to stay there anymore." I gave Cam a pointed look. He is going to give it away.

"Why not?" Graham asks from behind me. I laugh nervously as Cams eyes widened. "What's going on?" He asks.

"Let's go for a walk," I suggest to which he nods.

"Are you really going to tell him?" Cam asks.

"Yes, I don't really have a choice." He nods and Graham and I walk down the road.

"So tell me what's going on," he says a little impatiently. I'm obviously a big bundle of nerves at the moment.

"The cuts and bruises. They aren't from some stupid guy on the street," I admit.

He gives me a confused look. "You lied to me?" He asked obviously hurt.

"Yes, I had to. I didn't know what you would do if you found out." I explain, looking down.

"Who did this to you then? Don't-" he stopped abruptly. Turning to me he slowly started to figure things out. "The cuts and bruises. Cameron doesn't want you to go home. Who's hitting you?" He questioned.

He didn't know my step father was the only one I live with. "My step dad, Jay." It feels good to get off my chest for a second time. Now I can't tell anyone else.

"What? Why doesn't anyone stop him?" He yelled.

"It's only us, we live alone. After my mom died. Well you were there, but it's just us now. You can't tell anyone. Only you and Cameron know." I say and he jerks me too him.

"I'm so sorry, you can stay with me." He murmurs into my head. This isn't the reaction I was expecting. I hugged him back and he relaxed a little in my arms. "You can stay at my house if you need too."

"I'm okay, I'll be okay. It's just punishment for talking back and being late and things like that." I say and he looks at me like I'm crazy.

"No, it's abuse. You're being abused. I will protect you. I'll do whatever it takes to keep you safe." He declares fiercely. "You can stay at Cameron's or mine it doesn't matter as long as you're not there." I nod and we walk back to the house and Cameron was waiting by the door.

"Hey guys," Cameron says nonchalantly.

"Yes Cameron, I told him." I laugh a little.

"Oh," he says.

"So is that what you were talking about when you said that she would tell me on her own, I couldn't get mad and all that?" Graham asked. Cameron's eyes widen.

"What exactly did you say?" I asked and he smiled sheepishly.

"I just didn't want him to hurt you," he says and I hug him. He seem confused as he hugs me back.

"Thanks for looking out for me." I hug him tightly.

"No problem, shorty." He says with a smile. Suddenly a cop car pulled up and Andy came out. He walked up to me and his eyes widen.

"What the hell happened to you?" He asks.

"Some random guy on the street." I reply.

"You're not going to file a report?" He questioned suspiciously.

"I didn't get a good look." I lie again.

"Right," he replies not believing a word I say. Probably because they are lies. "Anyways did Jay tell you the news?"

"Um, no what's up?" I ask tilting my head. Graham and Cameron came and stood beside me.

"We found out who the truck belonged to." He explains, I nearly scream.

"What who?" I ask quickly. He give me a look of pity. I hate that look.

"We talked to him and he said that his truck went missing the same day of the crash. It was missing in the morning when he went to leave for work." He informs me. When he sees my face fall he tries to make me feel better. "We are so close. It won't take much more to find out who did this to your mom. You'll get your justice." He assures.

I smile and mumble an okay before Cameron hugs me again. "Thank you," I say and he smiles.

"I'm glad to help. Why didn't Jay tell you?" He questions.

"I wasn't home for a while and when I was home, he must have just forgot." I lie and look down. Graham rubs my back as he keeps his eyes on Andy. "Okay, thank you Andy."

"No problem. I'll let you know if I find out anything else." He smiles genuinely to me before nodding to the boys and walking back to his car, taking off.

"Was that the cop from the scene of the crime?" Graham asks.

"Yeah, that's him." I say turning to him.

"Since when do you call him by his first name?" He questions bitterly.

"Since he told me to." I answer, confused. "What's wrong?"

"Nothing," he murmurs as he stomps into Cameron's house.

"He's just jealous." Cameron shrugs and I look at him as he explains. "He thinks you have a thing for that cop. He doesn't know you like him."

"Oh," is all I could say as I follow him into his house.

Graham is sat on the couch flipping through the channels. "What movie do you want to watch?" He asks Cameron who just points to a random action movie. Cameron makes sure I'm sat beside Graham when we get situated for the movie.

After about an hour of the movie I begin to get extremely tired. My head falls on something that I soon recognize as Graham's shoulder. Frankly, I don't care. I'm tired and even if he's mad at me, it feels nice. I like him. I really like him.

This contact makes my stomach erupts in butterflies. It doesn't help when his fingers brush against my cheek. Next his thumb and then what I believe is his lips. I can feel his warm breath against my cheek. I already know I'm blushing as I open my eyes. He is facing me. His eyes piercing through mine, because the swelling had gone down and I could actually see. He leaned over and kisses my cheek.

"I'm sorry for getting angry, I was just jealous." He whispers in my ear. I blush and put my head in his chest.

"It's okay," I forgive him and then close my eyes as I fall asleep.

"Goodnight," he says quietly.

I wake up in Graham's arms for the second time. I could get used to this feeling. "We have school!" Cameron yells as we get ready.

When we make it to the school we enter together. Earning weird stairs from everyone around us. The day went by quickly and I got lots of weird looks and questions about what happened. If only they knew. Adrienne and Brianna have bugged me all day. Their reactions were normal but now they won't leave me alone, insisting that I had to know what happened. I don't know what to tell them.

I walk home after school. Yes home, only to get my things then I'm headed to Cameron's again. I pack up some outfits and other necessities. I quickly and quietly leave before Jay can notice I'm there. Then I make my journey to Cams.

My phone starts to ring and I pick it up, seeing that it's Cameron. "Hello?" I answer.

"We have a problem." He admits immediately.

Chapter 19

"What is it?" I sigh. I bet I already know what's going on.

"You can't stay the night." He informs me. Bingo, I knew it! "My parents are home and if I had a girl sleeping in my bedroom with me they'd flip. I'm sorry, I'm still not ready to tell them that I'm gay. You can see if you can stay with Graham tonight." He says and I smile.

"Yeah okay," I reply.

"I'm sorry, Reese." He apologizes again.

"It's fine," I laugh. I'll just call Graham and ask if I can stay with him tonight. "Okay, bye!"

"Bye," then he hung up. I wonder if Mike would be into Cam? Mike is a friend from my old school. We still keep in touch but it's been a while.

I'll call him and see if he wants to meet up. I quickly press call on his contact. It rings and rings. "How's my girl?" Mike nearly yells through the line.

"I'm great, how are you?" Yes because a black eye with cuts and bruises all over my body is just great!

"I'm doing awesome, I was going to call you the other day but I forgot. Do you wanna hang out sometime?" He asks, wow that was easier than I thought.

"Yeah, that's actually why I called. I also want you to meet someone." I slyly add and hear him sigh.

"Who is it this time?" He already knows what's coming.

"His name is Cameron. He's a really close friend. I think you've met him once before when you came to visit." I say and he laughs.

"I don't remember. The only thing I remember from that visit was the movie marathon." He said to me.

"Of course you do," I mutter.

"What?" He asks but I already know he heard me.

"Nothing, I just want you to meet him. I really think you'll like him!" I try and convince him and it works.

"Okay but this is the last time." He says warningly. I squeal and he laughs again. "How's this weekend?" He asks and I smile wildly.

"It's perfect! Okay I have to call a friend and see if I can stay at his house." I say and he coughs.

"His house? Who's this guy?" He asks suggestively.

"Just a friend, for now." I add for his amusement.

"Okay, tell your mom I said hi." He doesn't know. I forgot to tell him.

"Um, Mike. There was an accident and mom passed away." I explained, the line went silent.

"I'm sorry, I really liked her." He admitted and I smiled at that.

"It's okay, I have to go I'll talk to you later." I say quickly.

"I'll see you this weekend girl," he bids me farewell then I hang up.

Now I need to call Graham and see if I can stay there for the night. If not then it looks like I'm staying home. Adrienne is visiting her grandfather in Georgia for the week. So we can't hang out until next week. I miss Adrienne, I can't wait to go shopping with her.

I call Graham's cell and a female voice picks up. "What?"

"Is Graham there?" I ask hesitantly.

"No he's busy. Why are you calling him?" She seems snippy. I soon recognize the voice.

"Holly?" I question in return.

"No, it's Graham's other girlfriend. Yes it's Holly," She confirms. Graham's girlfriend? Oh, I understand.

"He just left his book at my house. I-I was just wondering when he wanted me to bring it back." I lied and she scoffed.

"Whatever, just don't call my boyfriend again!" She snapped. I could hear snickers from the other end of the line. Then she hung up. Well then, I'll just stay home. I headed back inside.

I sat on the couch watching a movie. Suddenly I hear the door click. It can't be Jay he would slam it. To my surprise He walks out with two different bags in hand. He is trying to be quiet, something's up. "What are you doing here?" He asked, shocked.

"Cameron canceled," I explain. He growls under is breath. I had told him I was saying at Cameron's for a while. Of course I told him over the phone.

"Okay well I'm tired. Goodnight," he rushes out before walking very fast up the stairs. That was extremely weird.

I finish watching my movie and then take a shower. After that it's school time. I didn't sleep a wink. I was too scared to sleep. I kept thinking that he would come down and try and hurt me again. I can't even feel safe in my own home.

"My friend Mike is coming down to visit this weekend." I tell Cameron with a smirk, sliding in beside him. Lunch was officially my favorite part of the day. He just rolls his eyes.

"I hope he knows that I'll be there." Cameron looks at me warily.

"He knows," I say shaking my head. Of course he knows, I wouldn't try and set them up unless I thought he would like him or he knew he was going to be there. "I can't wait until you guys fall in love."

"We will not fall in love," he protests.

"I'm telling you, you guys will hit it off." I told him and then Brianna walked up with a small smile.

"Hey guys," she says as she sets her tray down beside Cameron.

"Hey," we say simultaneously. "So, what did you guys do last night?" Cameron asked us and I dropped my head.

"What?" She asked with a laugh, completely confused.

Cameron's dark eyes turned to me. "You went home didn't you?" He questioned darkly. I'm in trouble.

"Cameron I had to. There wasn't anyplace else I could stay." I defended myself.

"Really, where was Graham? He said that he would let you stay with him whenever you needed to." He pointed out and I started to avoid eye contact.

"He was busy," I muttered. I notice Brianna go still behind him for a moment. Then, she starts to fidget uncomfortably.

"I'll just have to talk with him, but you should have just called me back. I would have worked something out." Cameron seems to notice how Brianna is acting as well. "What's up with you?"

"Oh um, nothing. Hey Graham said that you could just give his school book to me because I need to use it anyways." She replied, obviously trying to change the topic. I nodded at first.

Then my head snapped up at her. "Wait what?"

"I said that Graham said to just give me his book instead." She says uneasily.

"I don't have his book. I lied to Holly when she answered Graham's phone. I didn't want her to know I was calling to ask to stay the night. I mean she's his girlfriend, It would have been wrong and awkward." I explained and narrowed my eyes at her.

Cameron automatically glares at Brianna and she looks down in shame. "Graham was in the shower and I had Holly over to stay the night. We decided to sneak into his room and pull a prank. Then you called, Holly said it would be a harmless prank. I just went along with it. So she answered and told you they were dating. I didn't even know what she was going to say, I swear. After everything was said and done I felt bad but I didn't say anything because I didn't want you to be mad at me." She informed me and Cameron looked over to me.

"That's what he was busy with. You thought he was with Holly so you didn't stay with him. You were obviously hurt by it seeing as you like him." Cameron says making me roll me eyes. "Then you went home. So this is your fault." He said turning to Brianna.

"I didn't do it Holly did." She tried but Cameron wasn't about to let her get away with it.

"No, she would have stayed with him if it wasn't for you. You could have stopped her, but you didn't. You let her do it and Reese went home." Cameron accuses her. She tries to stand up for herself but Cameron was obviously pissed. He grabbed my arm and stomped away from her. I sent her an apologetic look.

Once we were out of the cafeteria Cameron pulled me into a hug. "Cameron, she doesn't even know what she did. She doesn't know about what's going on. That was rude." I say to him and he just hugs me tighter.

"I'm sorry," He murmurs.

You know what. I think I'm gong to tell Adrienne about what's happening. I mean she's my best friend. Cameron knows and if I told anyone else willingly it would be Adrienne. I would have told her and Cameron at the same time. They would be the first to know. Now Graham does.

"Reese?" Cameron whispers. I look up at him. "You just looked a little out of it."

"I've decided to tell Adrienne. I'll tell her when she gets back from her grandpa's." I tell him and he smiles widely.

"Finally!" He all but yells. "I knew you'd tell her sometime." I smile at him and then I heard a door open and Graham steps out of the cafeteria.

"What happened?" He asked and stepped up to Cameron and I.

"Just a misunderstanding." I admit and he gives me a tired look.

Cameron decides to tell him the story. "My parents came home and said that I couldn't have any friends over, let alone a girl. So I told her to call you instead. When she called, Holly answered. She told Reese that you too were dating and to stop calling. Reese panicked and lied about some book she needed to return. You were in the shower and they were going to pull a prank. Instead they saw who was calling and Holly decided to prank her, convincing Brianna that it was harmless. They did the prank and Reese thought it would be awkward if she did stay. Not to mention Holly would have said no. So she went home."

He was cut off by Graham. "You went home? You shouldn't have done that. You should have called back and asked to speak to me."

"I just thought you guys were dating and it would have been weird and caused problems." I admitted and his eyes softened a little.

"You know it's not true though?" He asked and I nodded. "She stays with Brianna all the time. I told you not to believe anything that she says."

"I'm sorry," I mumble and he pulls me to him.

"You know I don't want her right?" Graham asks into my hair.

"Yeah, you've said it a lot." I laugh and he sighs.

"Well I just wanted you to know, that will never happen. I can't stand her," he says and I smile slightly. "I care about you too much to ever do that to you." He whispers so that I couldn't hear but I did. I heard it and it made my day. My smile widened and I hugged him tightly.

"I have something to tell you guys." I announce stepping away so I can face both of the boys. "Jay was acting really weird last night. He was being secretive but that's a given because he always is. He didn't hit me. He didn't even yell at me. It was almost normal. I think he's done." I inform them and they both frown deeply.

"I don't think he is, Reese. Maybe he's just trying to fool you," Cameron states.

"I still don't like the fact that you stayed home. You are staying with me tonight. No questions asked." Graham gave me no room to talk. "I'll come and help you pack because I don't want you there alone."

"Graham, I'm already packed. I just don't think that I should stay with you." I tell him and he glares.

"You are, I don't trust him and I want you to be safe. Cameron's parents are going to be home and mine don't care so you're staying." He demands and I nod silently. I don't want to argue with him.

"I'll see you at your house then," I say as I move to go to class. You have science with him. The voice inside my he's patronizes me.

"You'll come?" He asked hopefully. I nod again and he smiles. "Are you going to walk?"

"Yeah I'll just come around seven, if that's okay." I add but he was to busy in his own little world to notice what I said.

"Absolutely," he murmurs before almost skipping off.

I ring the door bell and wait for an answer. A woman in her late thirties answers the door. "Oh, another one of Brianna's friends? I didn't know she was having more than one." She asked, giving me a strange look. She's staring at my black eye. Plus the bruises.

"Oh um, actually Brianna and I-" I stopped and decided to skip that part. She didn't need to know about that. "Actually, I'm a friend of Graham's." I admit shyly.

"I see," she smiled sweetly. "Please come in." She seems incredibly nice.

"Thank you," I take her offer and step in. It's a pretty house. "Did you decorate?" I ask and she smiles.

"Yes, I did. Do you like it?" She says proudly.

"Yes, I wish my house looked like this." I tell her with a look of disgust as I think back to my house. The empty beer cans and bottles of different varieties everywhere. The blood stains on the carpet and walls. It's bad, and I just cleaned it not too long ago.

"I could come over and help you decorate sometime," She's very polite but now I'm going to panic.

"No, it's okay." I reply a little to quickly. She notices and gives me a weird look. Luckily she brushes it off and hollers for Graham to come. "Thank you, you're very nice." I say and she smiles even wider.

"You are a very polite young lady." She compliments.

"I'm just not used to people being so nice. I'm trying to return the favor."

She give me a confused look. "Why?"

Oh no, how am I going to explain this? Just as I open my mouth to come up with some lie, Graham grabs my hand. "What are you ladies talking about?" He asks and I look down.

"Just girl stuff," she replies.

"Mom, don't embarrass me!" He whines.

She laughs and hugs him. "I like her, she's a lot better than that Holly girl that likes you so much." His mom says into his ear and he blushes. Awe, so cute. Wait, why is he blushing?

"Well, let's go up stairs." He begins to pull me but his mom stops him.

"What's your name?" She asks me.

"Reese," I respond and she smiles. Suddenly a man that looks almost like an older version of Graham comes up beside her.

"That's a beautiful name." She compliments and the man puts an arm around her waist.

"Reese, what?" Who I'm guessing is Graham's father asks for my last name. "I might know your parents."

"Fode, my dad's name is John and my moms name was Madeline." I say and his wife's eyebrows furrow.

"Was?" She asks.

"Mom," Graham warns.

"No, it's okay." I tell him. "My mom died in a car accident, last month actually."

His mom covered her mouth as she gasped and his father went rigid. "I'm sorry," they say in unison.

"I'm taking Reese up to my room." Graham replies a little angrily. He jerks me up the stairs and into his bedroom. Man what's his problem?

His bedroom is big. There is a large bed in the middle and the room is pretty plain. He must have taken down all the inappropriate posters before I came. I laugh at the thought if him running around like a mad man trying to hide everything.

We hear a voice call, "how long is your friend staying Graham?" It was his mom.

He groans and yells back, "All night!"

"Come down here son we need to have a talk." His dad yells up at him.

"Bring your friend too," his mom adds.

"Come on," he mutters pulling me down the steps once more. I toss my bag in before he does so. Once we reach the bottom of the stairs we walk to the kitchen table where his parents are seated. "Yes?"

"I'm going to allow her to sleep in your room. However, there are rules. She can't sleep in your bed with you." His father starts but his wife cuts in.

"She can sleep in the bed. You can sleep on the floor." Graham's mom says as she smiles at me. I smiled back.

"My parents like you more than me." Graham whispers in my ear.

"You have to keep the door open and you can't have sex." His father declares bluntly. I choke on my own spit and Graham turns beat red.

"Dad!" He yells. "I can't believe you just said that."

"Well I'm just covering all the bases," his father shrugs.

"Okay, this is awkward. Agreed, we are going now." Graham says grabbing my hand once again.

"Wait, do you guys want snacks?" His mom asks and he shakes his head as he continues up the flight of stairs. "Okay, have fun."

Graham grumbles something as we make our way to his room. He leaves the door cracked then he plops down on his bed. He looks at me as I stand there awkwardly and pats his bed. I sit down beside him. After a while he wraps his arms around my waist and pulls me back, making me squeal. He sets me on my back and lays down beside me. He shoots me one of his dazzling smiles.

"So talk to me," he says.

"What do you want me to talk about?" I ask and he shakes his head.

"You don't even have to talk. Just lay there." He mumbles but I understand it. I give him a confused look and he smiles even wider as he stares at me. "You're so beautiful."

I blush insanely and he kisses my cheek. "Stop," I push his face away and he laughs.

"You're just so cute and amazing," he mumbles. I blush again and his face moves closer to mine. If I was to move an inch forward we would be kissing. He put his hands on my face and cupped my cheeks, slowly moving forward. Our lips brush and I'm about to close the space when the door bursts open. I shove myself away from him and glance up at who had barged in. Graham groans out in frustration and I just look away with a blush on my face.

Chapter 20

(Graham's POV)

"What's going on in here?" Brianna gave Reese a knowing look. I'd like to know the same.

"What is she doing here, with you?" Holly asked in a tone of disgust.

I'm so angry right now! My little sister and her whore of a friend just ruined the perfect moment. We were about to kiss! She was going to close the space! I almost got to kiss the girl of my dreams. I was so close. That was our second almost kiss. I'm going to kill my little sister.

Now I have three reasons to kill both Holly and Brianna. For one she just did that! She ruined it, but I will get my kiss. She also pulled that prank on Reese, who was seemingly upset when she thought I was with Holly. Which made me weirdly happy. Plus she snuck into my room without me knowing, invading my privacy. They both deserve what's coming to them.

I looked over to Reese and her cheeks were an adorable shade of red. She is avoiding any eye contact in the room as she looks out the window. Wow, she's beautiful. I can imagine what it would be like if we were to kiss. We could watch some of her movies and cuddle. We could fall asleep together. Oh wait, we already did that. I think with a smirk. I snap back to reality and glare harshly at my sister. "Get out," I growl at them.

"Why is she here?" Holly asks again and I move my glare to her.

"She's staying the night with me. In my room, alone." I smirk at her and I see Brianna suppressing her smile.

Holly's jaw drops as she stares at me. I look over at Brianna and she is looking at Reese with an apologetic expression. Then, she speaks. "I'm so sorry, Reese. I'll make it up to you." Brianna says sincerely. Reese just smiles at her and then looks down.

"Why does she have to stay here?" Holly complained. I wanted to blow up on her so badly. I wanted to tell her that she has to or she'll be beaten for some stupid reason. "I mean she can just go home."

I stand up from the bed and get up in her face. "No, she's staying with me because I don't want her to go home. I want her safe and within arms reach." I snap and then Reese walked up to me.

She gently placed a hand on my arm and pulled lightly. I looked down at her pleading eyes and I sat back down on the bed. Reese stayed standing so I pulled her down with me, causing her to gasp. I smile at her and she smiles back shyly.

"Well mom wants you and your friend down for dinner." Brianna says with a smile but her eyes give away her confusion. Holly rolls her eyes as she stomps out of the room.

"Come on," I smile warmly at Reese as I reach my hand out for her to take. She does and we walk down the stairs hand in hand. Once we reach the bottom, my mom smiles warmly at us and smirks at our conjoined hands. Reese jerks her hand back from mine quickly and I sigh, missing the contact.

The table was set and the food was already served out. I don't understand what's going on. We never have dinner when we have friends over. Unless it's my parents and it a business dinner or something. Other than that we just good off and eat popcorn. My mom was offering Reese a seat beside her and when she went to take it I pulled her away to sit by me.

After half an hour we finish our food. "Did you like the meal, Reese?" My mother asked her with hopeful eyes.

"Yes it was amazing. You have to teach me how to make that steak." Reese replied much to my surprise. I thought she would just smile and nod.

My mom was absolutely glowing now. "Absolutely, you just call and come over anytime!"

"Mom, why did you make dinner?" I asked her and her turned to me.

"I just wanted to impress your friend." She admits and I sigh.

"You didn't need to mom. She likes you already," I mumble. My mom turns back to Reese as she whispers something over the table. I didn't catch it but Reese giggles and looks at me.

This dinner was terrible. Don't get me wrong, the meal was great. It was amazing actually, but there was so much tension. My mom wanted to please Reese. Reese wanted to please both my parents. Holly was glaring daggers into Reese the whole dinner. Brianna kept making comments in my ear about how much I liked Reese and what we were going to do tonight. Then she'd threaten me about hurting her. My dad was just a complete mess. He was very nervous and extra polite to everyone except Holly. She was constantly wanting my parens approval and opinion. She wanted them to like her but they didn't. They could see right through her facade. They really liked Reese though. They could tell she was sweet and kind, everything Holly was not. That's pissed Holly off, majorly. I had a feeling she would try to mess this night up, but I won't let her.

"Do you want to watch a movie?" I asked Reese, interrupting her chat with my mom. My dad was officially avoiding everyone. He tried not to talk which is weird because he was a very talkative person.

"Sure, see you later Mrs. Winters." She says waving to my mom as I tug her up the stairs. Once again I leave the door open a crack.

Stupid parents.

I understand where they're coming from though. I wouldn't trust a teenage boy in a room alone with a beautiful, sexy girl like Reese either. God, how's she so amazing?

I slip in a random movie and we watch the whole thing. Neither of us are tired and I said I was going to make popcorn. She smiled as she went through my movies. I walk down stairs and hear the faint voices of my parents.

"I told you, I was out with the guys." They were arguing. It's funny, they always fight in the kitchen.

"You've said that at least one day every weekend. I talked to Jimmy, he said you only go out every other weekend. Are you seeing somebody else?" My mothers hurt voice accuses.

That would explain a lot. He is cheating on my mom. That's why he is acting so weird. That's what he meant when he said that he'd messed up. There goes my happy family. It still doesn't compare to Reese's family. It just makes me mad to think about it.

A minute later it sounded like he was about to reply when the stair creaked. Seriously, now you creak? I step into the kitchen and look up at them like I hadn't known what was going on. "I came for some popcorn." I point to the cabinet. I soon notice my moms tear stained face and my fathers hurt expression.

"Okay sweetheart, make it then you guys need to go to bed soon. It's a school night." My mom sniffled then walked out wiping her eyes. I do as she says.

When I go up stairs I make a bed on the floor and lay down on it. Reese hovers over me. "Get up," she whispers. As I stand up I look her from head to toe. Her hair was pulled into a messy bun and her shirt was a black one with a blue circle that said Evanescence. Her shorts were the shortest I'd seen on her. They looked hot. They barley covered her butt and they were black as well. Only they said Aero on the hip. The scars didn't even faze me.

She pushed me down on my bed and laid down on the floor. I glared down at her but it vanished as soon as I saw her. She was looking at me adoringly and she had a small smile playing at her lips. "I'm not letting you sleep on the floor," I say stubbornly. She pouts and I sigh, "Whatever."

Once I see she starts to fall asleep. I lay down next to her. Her wide eyes snap to mine. "What are you doing? Your dad said that-"

"Shh," I cut her off by running my thumb along her bottom lip. "He said that we couldn't sleep together in my bed. This isn't my bed."

She looks at me warningly but soon gives in and cuddles up to me. I reach down and trace her scars with my fingers. She shivers sometimes, but I only go over them again and again. I think they are beautiful. Not the story behind them or how they got there. Normally I would. I would love the story but I already know and these are horrible. I just love them because they are a part of her. No matter how they got there, she makes them beautiful.

"Will you tell me about your scars?" I ask quietly.

"You already know how they got there." She mumbles, obviously tired.

"I want to know their stories, please?" I beg and she sighs nodding. "This one," I trace over it. It was the longest one on her leg. It ran from her calf to the upper back of her thigh.

"He slapped my mom right in front of me for the first time. I threw one of his empty beer bottles at his face but he dodged it. Then he came after me with a large shard of the glass. I tried to run like my mom told me to, but I tripped. I tried to squirm away but he stabbed my thigh and dragged it down my leg. My mom just stood there and watched. I couldn't walk for a week. It hurt to much." She told me the story and my grip on her tightened. It was like if I let her go she would be hurt again.

My curiosity got the best of me as I ran my fingers up her back and she arched it. Causing her chest to dig into mine. "And this one?" I questioned breathlessly, running my three middle fingers about an inch left of her spine. It ran all the way up to the top of her shoulder blade.

She shivered again under my touch. "He had a couple of his work partners over and I embarrassed him in front of all his friends so he took me into his room and sliced my back open. There are a couple from the same time." I'd had enough of the stories as I rolled her over onto my chest. She audibly gasped.

"Go to sleep," I order and she didn't hesitate.

Around three in the morning she starts to shake and turn a little on me, waking me up. She whimpers and digs her nails into my chest. She gasps and her eyes squeeze tight. Then she starts breathing heavily, very heavily. Then it quickens and I realize what's happening. She's having a bad dream, and it's causing her to have a panic attack in her sleep. She lets out a shrill scream and it was loud enough to wake anyone in this house. I shake her shoulders and she screams again. I shake her roughly and she opens her eyes widely gasping for air. I sit up, holding her shaking body against me as I whisper things into her ear to try and calm her down.

I rub the arm that's not pressed against me in attempt to soothe her. She's sobbing into my chest. "He-He-," I struggle to quiet her. Then everyone came running into the room. "H-he came, I-It was so r-real. H-he h-hurt you. I t-tried to help y-you. He was j-just too strong. P-please forgive me?" She begged and sobbed.

"Okay baby, you're okay. He's not here, he won't hurt you." I tried to comfort her. I know she was more worried about him hurting me by the way she explained it. My mom looked at her in panic.

She slowly approached us. "Honey, do you want to go home?" Reese tensed automatically. She shook her head no at first then she nodded. Now it was my turn to be tense. "Okay let's get your-" I cut my mom off.

"No, you're not going home. You're staying with me." I demanded but she looked up at me. She looked so broken, so hurt. It must have been terrible for her.

"I need to go home," she tells me and I furrow my eyebrows. "That way I can make sure he stays there. You'll be safe."

"But you won't be, you'll be the one in danger." I nearly yelled, completely forgetting about our audience. I don't care if they know. I think it's better if they do. Reese is the one that afraid to tell anyone. "You're staying here with me!"

"Graham if I go home then I can make sure he's there and keep you safe, like I said before. You'll be okay. That's all I care about," she says sincerely. I wanted to kiss her so bad right now. I new that wouldn't be the best choice as my parents are right there. Also I can tell they are confused as hell.

"If you go, it'll drive me crazy thinking about you! I need to know you're safe and the only way is if you stay with me. If you got hurt again then I don't know what I'd do. I need you, Reese. I need you to be safe because I can't stand the thought of him touching you again! I care about you way to much to let you leave," I confess. It felt so good to say but It didn't clear away all of it. I want to tell her I like her but now is not the time.

She stares at me awestruck. Still sitting in my lap with tears running down her face and her arms around him neck. She hugs me tightly and I savor the feeling of her in my arms. "I'll stay," she squeaks out cutely. My tense body relaxes a little at her words.

"What the hell is going on?" Everyone yells, even Holly. She didn't look angry anymore just confused along with everyone else.

I panic again but Reese seemed to have this under control. "Remember that guy I told you about? The one that did all this?" She asks Brianna pointing to her black eyes and bruises. She nods and Reese continued. "Well, he lives with my step dad. He's our cousin Jeremiah."

Everyone got understanding looks in their faces and Reese hid in my chest. Sniffling every couple seconds. "She had a bad dream where he came and hurt me," I elaborated and everyone soon left the room, except my mom. She stayed behind for a moment.

"I'm sorry, Reese. I was wondering what had happened to you. That's terrible. Feel free to stay whenever," my mother offers before leaving.

Reese turns to me and gives me a sad smile. "Do you rally have a cousin named Jeremiah?" I ask and she shakes her head no. "That was quick thinking." I mutter and she snuggles up to me. "He won't touch you again," I whisper and she falls off to sleep.

The rest of the night I was on edge. I wanted her to be safe and with me at all times now. After her dream, it gave me bad thoughts. Like her step dad coming and hurting her. I feel like I can't protect her unless she's with me and that's all I want to do. My parents would peak in every once in a while and check on her mostly. I wasn't going to let her out of my sight from now on. So when my dad saw Reese on the floor wrapped up in my arms he didn't even say anything. He just let it be.

Soon my alarm went off and I had to slap at it. It stopped buzzing and I looked down to Reese. Her beautiful brown eyes are staring up at me. They were still a little puffy from the crying but beautiful nonetheless. She snuggled into my chest again and sighed. "We have school in an hour," I say into her hair. She gets up and walks over to the bathroom. Then I hear the shower running. "I have to get ready too you know."

"Okay then get ready," she replies. I slowly open the door and step in. I could see her shadow behind the curtain but that was it. "Get ready but don't pull the curtain back or I'll punch you." She threatens and I laugh. I leave my hair alone, letting it be messy. I just don't have the energy for it today. I wash the sleepiness from my face. Then brush my teeth and go back into the room. I pick out a simple plain black shirt and a pair of jeans. Basically the first things I pull out of my closet. Then I walk back into the bathroom. I spray my cologne and then the water shuts off. "Hey can you hand me a towel?"she asks.

"Yeah sure," I respond tossing a white towel over the curtain. I hear her mumble a thanks before I walk back into the bedroom. I shove all my books back into my school bag and zip it up. I see bare feet on the floor a couple feet away. My eyes slowly trail upwards. Sexy bare legs, a white cloth that covers from her mid-thigh to her chest, which had little specks of water on it and her shoulders to, her hair was soaking wet as it laid against her back. Her hand was holding the fabric tightly to her chest.

"I-I need my bag." She stutters shyly, closing the door behind her. I'm gawking at her and I know it but I can't look away.

"Uh-What?" I ask dumbly. What am I doing? Be cool dude! "Oh yeah, here." I hand her bag to her.

"Thank you," she says and stares at me just as I do the same to her. "Could you, um, turn around so I can get dressed?" She questions awkwardly.

"Oh! Oh, I'm sorry!" I quickly turn around and hear her shuffling. It's taking everything in me to not turn around. Her bag was already unzipped so when I hear the zipper I know she's closing it. Some more shuffling and then she walks in front of me. "Ready?"

"Yeah," she smiles up at me and I grab her hand and walk her out the door and into the car. Once we start to move I see her pull out a bag. Its makeup. She pulls out mascara and eye shadow those are the only things she puts on. Then she puts everything away again.

"Why do you only use mascara and eye shadow?" I question.

"It's just simple, everyone knows about my eye and lip so why hide it with consealer? If it's bad then yes I wear more to cover it up but other than that I just leave it." She explains and I nod curtly. "I'm sorry about the scare last night. I'll stay someplace else from now on."

"No you're staying with me. I want you safe and I'll protect you myself. It wasn't that big of a deal." I brushed her off and she smiles slightly. It scared the shit out of me that's all. I kissed her on the cheek and then helped her out of the car. She was blushing as I did so. She's so cute.

Ill protect her. I'll care for her, I'll be everything she needs. I'd do anything for this girl. Just as those thought cross my mind she kisses my cheek like I did to hers and drops her head walking away. I stood shocked for a second. Then a huge smile crossed my face and I ran up to her. I held her hand, our fingers intertwined, as we walked into the school.

CHAPTER 21

(Reese's POV)

School ended about an hour ago. Graham had spent every second he could with me. Which I was thankful for. I liked being around him. Probably because I like him.

When I was in nothing but a towel he was checking me out and it didn't bother me one bit. I just wanted to know what he thought of me. I wanted to know what he was thinking at that time. I guess I'll just have to find out myself.

I kick a rock as I make my way to the cemetery. I was visiting my moms grave. I made it a point to visit as often as I could, I'd update her on what was going in with my life. It was ridiculous that they didn't even have a funeral for her. They just buried her. Once I reach her grave I become confused. There are dozens of flowers that covered her headstone. Roses, daisies, and carnations. I hadn't put them there, so who did?

My moms grave that was once dull and bare is now colorful and bright because of the many flowers. Maybe Jay was the one who did it. I think he loved her, that would explain why he had cried when he found out she died. I'll just ask him. He's changed, when he saw me at home he didn't yell or hit me. He didn't even glare my way.

"Hey, mom." I greet the medium sized gravestone. "Who gave you all these flowers?"

Of course I got no answer, I mean, I'm talking to a stone. I just feel like she can hear me, like she's listening. She's always listen to me before. She'd listen to my problems and then give me advice. I just wish she was here and I'll always want that. I know she can't come back. I'm okay with that now because I've accepted her death. I will find out who did this to her and the baby. I want to hear their excuse as to why they did this, then fled the scene. I want to know if they are remorseful for what they've done. There are just a lot of unanswered questions.

"So there's this guy," I started. Yes, I was going to tell her about Graham. He was my only crush and he cared for me. I wanted to tell her I was being treated right, to let her know that I was okay. "His name is Graham. He's sweet and he's nice to me. He knows about Jay as well. He just wants to protect me. He's held me while I cried and he's helped me through hard times. We almost kissed, actually. I really wanted him to kiss me but his sister and her friend interrupted. I hope he kisses me soon though." I blush at the thought of his lips on mine.

I tell her all about the last month, some things I've already told her once before. I tell her about Adrienne and how I miss her. She's coming back in one day and as soon as she does we're going shopping and having a movie marathon. I talk for three hours as I sit at the foot of her grave.

Once I finish, I bid her farewell then I stand up to leave. There was a sound of rustling in the distance. I walk two steps towards the noise and squint my eyes trying to see better. I back away slowly, getting ready to turn and leave, when I see a head peak out from behind a tree. It was retracted quickly and my eyes widen as I turn and take off running. I dart through the trees as I take the short way out.

I didn't get a good look at the face but I saw they had short hair. Once I thought I was a safe distance away I slowed my pace. I walked all the way home to my house, which both Graham and Cameron would oppose to. When I step inside I see Jay passed out on the couch with his mouth open causing him to drool everywhere.

I walked into the basement and set my bag down. I was ready for a nap. My sleep last night was restless. Then I had the nightmare. I am so embarrassed about that. I'm such a weak person. I cried in Graham's arms until I fell asleep. Jays right, I am pathetic.

After about an hour nap I realized that I was starving. Jogging upstairs I saw that Jay was no longer sleeping either. I made some chicken and mashed potatoes. "Jay, are you hungry?" I call into the living room. He comes out into the kitchen.

"I was hungry six hours ago but you decided not to come home. Where the hell where you?" He asked angrily.

"I was visiting my mothers grave," I said. "Haven't you visited her?" I was thinking he would say yes so I could say he had no right to be mad.

"No, I haven't went at all!" He yelled at me and my face twisted in confusion.

"You didn't bring her a bunch of flowers?" I questioned and he shook his head in disgust.

"That whore was probably seeing someone else." He accused, which hit a nerve.

"Don't speak about my mother like that." I said though gritted teeth. His eyes widened and his nostrils flared with anger.

I soon realize he is advancing at me so I move and run into the living room. I reach for the door and open it but he shut it with his foot. "Where are you going? Back to you're boy toy? Poor guy doesn't even realize he's being used by a slut. You get it from your mom." He snarls at me, his proximity made me uncomfortable. He had me trapped against a door with his body. I was about to cry but I wouldn't give him that satisfaction.

His hands found my waist and he gripped so hard I was sure it'd leave a bruise. He pulled me until my body was pressed against his and then he slammed me against the front door with all his might, making my loose my breath momentarily. I gasped and tried to catch my breath. Resultantly, he smirked at what he'd done. "Stop," my voice was a lot stronger than I had expected.

He looked surprised to say the least. I then squirmed, stepping on his bare feet. He stumbled back and opened the door running out and to Cameron's house. He opened the door within seconds and he pulled me into a hug. I wasn't crying but he knew from the look on my face.

We were up in his room and he was trying to cheer me up. "So I bought you something." He said as he pulled out clay and an airbrush from his closet. I smiled and he gave me a hopeful look. I took them in my hands.

"Thank you," I say and he just shrugs. "Let's watch a movie!" I exclaimed. He laughed and brought out one of my favorite movies, The Exorcist.

We watched movies for hours on end. I got in the shower and then got ready for bed. We had two hours to sleep before we had to go to school. I passed out around five thirty so I had to get up in an hour.

By lunch time I was definitely ready to eat. I hadn't seen Graham until now and I can safely say that he has seen better days. He had bags under his eyes as if he hadn't slept all night. Once he saw me his eyes had brightened a little and I was pleased that I could have that effect on him. He sat down right next to me and kissed my cheek. I blushed and Cameron and Brianna smirked where as Adrienne looked completely shocked.

Adrienne came back this morning and she had missed a lot. I agreed to catch her up after school and told her we could go shopping. As Graham kissed my cheek she just looked utterly confused and happy at the same time. I smiled at her then turned to Graham. He was staring at me and when I caught him he quickly looked away. I laughed lightly and scratched my side. I went to pull my shirt back down but Graham grabbed my hand before I could. I follow his gaze down to my hips that have finger shaped bruises.

"Where did you stay last night?" He asks me softly and I shake my head.

"With Cameron," I assure and he believes me. I didn't think he would, I thought he'd have to check with Cameron first. I leaned forward to whisper in his ear. "He did it last night, before I went to Cams. I mouthed off." I explain and make sure no one heard. Luckily, no one did.

He grabbed my hand and kissed my scabbed knuckles. "I don't want you to go back anymore," he murmurs.

"I have to." I tell him an he closes his eyes.

"Just don't go there without me." He reasoned and my eyes widened as I shook my head furiously. "Please? He won't hurt me, I promise. He won't hurt you if I'm there."

If he gets hurt then I won't be able to live with myself. At the same time I want to believe what he said. "Okay," I said breathily and he smiled pulling my entire body to him and embracing me into a careful hug. I was basically sitting on his lap now. I notice people looking at us and giving us curious expressions.

"Ignore them," he whispers in my ear. I do as he says and then lunch was over.

School was quick and I went to the mall with Adrienne. I had to be back early because Mike was coming tomorrow. I already caught Adrienne up on the Graham drama and what not. She was pissed when I told her what Brianna and Holly did. Now I was going to tell her about Jay. "You know my step dad, Jay?" I asked her calmly.

"Yeah," she says as her eyebrows furrow.

"He hits me," I rushed out. She stares at me in complete shock. All the bags she had in her hands hit the ground and she stared analyzing my body.

"I'm sorry! I should have known! All the bruises and cuts. I'm so stupid." She yells looking at my faded black eye. My lip was completely healed except for the small scar left behind. I heal quickly, unless I pick at the scabs. I still had a little gash on my hip because it was so deep. Most of my bruises had healed up and my cuts too. I was healing pretty well.

"Is not your fault. I've been staying with Cameron and Graham so I haven't gotten it too bad lately." I try to convince her.

"You can stay with me anytime you need, you're my best friend. I can't believe I didn't figure it out," She exasperated. "Who else knows?"

"Too many people," I mutter. She gives me a tired look and I tell her. "Cameron, Graham and you." I answer and she nods.

"No one else?" She asks and I think about it for a minute.

"Well there's a chance that Andy knows. Although I didn't tell him." I say and she gives me a weird look.

"Who's Andy?" She asks and I mentally slap myself.

"Officer Menna," I elaborate. She gives me a look of bewilderment.

"The cop knows?" She all but yells.

"Well I didn't tell him but he probably does." She just shakes her head at me. After that we went to her house and watched Harry Potter. Then I went home.

I snuck in down stairs and took my shower. I got everything ready and then went to sleep. When I woke up I got ready and ran to meet Mike at the diner. When I arrive, he's already there. "Hey!" He exclaimed and I run up to hug him.

"What happened to your eye?" He asks pulling away.

"I was messing around with a friend and things got out of hand." I lied but he believed it and we went on our way. "We have to wait for Cameron." I say and he rolls his eyes.

Not five minutes later Cameron walks through the door. He was dressed up a little more than usual. He blonde hair was styled to perfection and he was wearing a grey shirt with some jeans. I look over and see Mike staring wide-eyed at him. I smirk and wave him over. He smiles showing off his slight dimples and I'm pretty sure Mike just audibly sighed. I laugh a little and Cameron sits down. "What's the plan?" He asks me.

"Cameron, this is Mike. Mike, this is Cameron." I introduce the two. Cameron turns to face Mike and his smile drops. I get confused for a moment. Then I realize what's happening.

They are both looking at each other with wide eyes. "H-hi," Cameron stutter and I smirk. They are going to get married. I think to myself.

Mike blushed and I'm reframing myself from squealing with joy. "I'm Mike," he says. Then blushed deeper and laughs nervously, "but you already knew that."

"I'm going to go to the restroom," I excuse myself but neither of them notice. I did well. I head over to the restroom and I see

Graham, Brianna, and Holly. She seems to be spending a lot of time with them lately.

I wash my hands and then I get ready to leave. I didn't have to use the restroom I just wanted to give them some time to theirselves. Just as I'm about to pass the table that Graham's was at I hear a whine, "Reese!" I can't help but laugh at Mike. He can be a child when he wants to be. He can also be intimidating. He's a very confusing character. "Why did you leave?" He pouts.

"I had to pee!" I exclaimed and he just laughed.

"Yeah right," he snorted out.

"Whatever," I admit. "You didn't even notice I was gone until now."

"He's just so cute," he pouts again and I just shove his shoulder.

"I told you, you'd like him." I whispered and he rolled his eyes. "I think he likes you too," I add.

His eyes filled with hope. "Really?"

"It's pretty obvious." I chuckle and he sighs.

"Let's eat and then go to the movies," He suggested.

"Hey, Reese." I hear a familiar voice say.

My smile grows wide as I look at Graham, "Hey." He doesn't look too happy as he stares Mike down. "Oh, Mike this is Graham. Graham, this is my friend Mike. We used to go to school together before I moved." I told them and they nodded to each other.

Mike smirked at me and I knew that this was going to be bad. "Was this the guy you were talking about on the phone?"

"Yes," I admitted and blushed. I look down to avoid any eye contact. I glanced up at Graham who had a large smile on his face as he looked at me.

"So you talk about me huh?" He teased only causing me to blush even more.

"That's Brianna," I pointed to her. Holly clears her throat and I raise a brow.

"I'm Holly," she says winking at him. I laugh loudly and Cameron comes up behind me. Mike takes a step back and everyone gives me confused looks.

"Um, I'm hungry." Mike says awkwardly I'm aware that it's because Holly is making him uncomfortable. I mean, he's gay and she's hitting on him.

"We can join you!" Holly said as she stood up from the table and walked over to our booth with Mike. Cameron was glaring at the back of her head and I patted his shoulder.

After we ate I was finding it funny that Holly was still hitting on Mike. Cameron was having no fun at all. Graham sat beside me and kept touching me. Whether it was holding my hand or kissing my cheek. I just watched in amusement as Holly went to kiss Mike and he shoved her face away.

"Just tell them," I say and he looks up and nods. He's already came out about being gay. Cameron was the one who hasn't.

"I'm gay, so back off." He said moving to sit by Brianna.

Graham lets out a breath. "I was nervous you'd make a move on my girl." He joked and I laughed as well as everyone else at the table. Mine wasn't whole hearted though. It actually kind of hurt.

"Don't be nervous sweetie. No one can take me from you." Holly winked and Graham looked confused. His mouth made an O shape and he turned to me.

"I was actually talking about Reese." He said quietly then his eyes widened and he started shaking his head. "Not that you're my girl. If you don't want to be. We never said we were going to be anything other than friends. I know you don't like me like that." He rambled nervously.

I blushed deeply at his words. He called me his girl. Then he took it back and said that I didn't like him like that. I can't believe he doesn't see right through me. I suck at hiding my feelings.

Cameron snorts and Graham looked at him. His cheeks still a rosy color. "You're stupid," Cameron tells him. I slap his chest but he just shrugs.

"How am I stupid?" He asked and I sink down in my seat. Holly is officially planing my death by the look she is giving me.

"It's pretty obvious, dude." Mike says looking at me and then back to Graham.

"Someone please tell me why I'm stupid!" He demands.

"Reese-" Mike starts but I cut him off.

"We're going to be late for the movie." I talk over him and he smirks.

"We don't even know which movie we are going to see." Mike points out and I blush getting up from my seat.

"Well, I wouldn't want to be late for it." I said lamely.

Both Cameron and Mike smile at me and we take our leave. However, before I can walk away Graham grabs my arm. "Are you staying with me tonight?"

"If you want me to," I hint shyly.

"I really do," he whispers back. I smile brightly and nod.

"I'll be a little late though, if that's okay." I add hesitantly.

"Of course, I'll see you then." He says kissing my cheek. I blush and then follow the boys to the car.

CHAPTER 22

I step into the living room. Mike and Cameron had gotten along when they met. They really liked each other. I can't wait until they get together and I'm right. Now Mike and I are having a movie marathon, even though we just got back from the movies. We're currently watching X Men: First Class. We are nerds.

"I have to go home. My mom doesn't want me to stay the night so I have to be back by ten. I should leave now to get there on time." Mike says standing up. Then he smirks and turns to me. "By the way, you were right. I like Cameron. He's cute and funny and just overall amazing."

"Glad to hear you admit it." I mumble and he raises his brows. "He liked you too." I told him and he smiled.

"He's coming over to my place on Friday and staying all weekend." He says proudly as he walks confidently over to the door.

"I knew it!" I shout and he laughs.

"Graham obviously likes you." He points out causing me to blush.

"I can't believe you and Cameron almost told him I like him! It would have been so awkward!" I yell, hitting him in the arm.

"I can't believe you haven't yet!" He retorts. "He needs to know. He likes you too."

"Are you sure? I don't know, he probably just thinks of me as a friend." I say sadly. His eyes almost pop out of his skull.

"Are you serious?" He yells in my ear. I nod and he continues. "He was all over you at lunch. He called you his girl and then got nervous. He kissed your cheek, for crying out loud!" He exclaims and I blush.

"Yeah, I'll tell him how I feel soon." I say and he smiles.

"I'll talk to you later, goodbye." He hugs me, walking out the door to his car and taking off.

I gather a couple outfits and put them in my bag. I get some makeup, body wash, etc. I sling my bag over my shoulder and head over to Graham's. Mike lives an hour and a half away so he'll be home by ten. It's currently eight thirty. I'll start walking to Graham's and I should be there by nine.

I start walking and I make it there a little later than I had expected. Its only nine thirty but still. I knock and wait patiently. When the door opens I come face to face with Mr. Winters. "Oh hi, come in."

"Thanks," I say and he smiles awkwardly at me. Graham comes into view and he smiles at me, wrapping me up in his arms.

"Hey," he mumbles into my hair. I giggle and he takes me up to his room. "I didn't think you were going to come. Who drove you?" He asks once we reach his room.

"I walked, that's why I was late." I explained and he sat me down on his bed.

"You could have just called me. I would have came and got you. My mom is here so I could have used her car." He offered and I nodded to him.

"Thanks, I'll ask next time." I agreed and he smiled. Slight dimples showing on his cheeks. He's very attractive. His light blue eyes with little specks of green were staring into mine. His lips were parted enough to show his white teeth. I was close enough to see a little stubble on his cheeks. How can someone so good looking with such a big heart care for someone like me?

"Why are you staring at me?" He asks with a laugh. I hadn't even realized I was. I blush and look into his eyes.

"Your just..." I trail off, blushing deeper. His smile drops and his face inches closer to mine.

"I'm just what?" He asks. I can feel his breath on my lips and cheeks.

The door opened and his mom stepped in. I jerked my head away from his and moved off the bed. "Oh, sorry for interrupting. I just wanted to tell you that I made some sandwiches." She said, blushing herself at what she just walked in on.

She pulled out a tray of what looks like turkey sandwiches. Graham walks over with a sigh. He takes the tray and sets it on the table. "Thanks mom," he murmurs.

His mom walks out and he turns to me. A small smirk playing at his lips. I give him a wary look and his smirk grows. "Moment lost?" He asked.

"A little," I say and he sighs.

"Oh well then," if his smirk grows anymore his handsome face will break. He runs at me and tackles me to the bed, making me squeal. He tickles at my sides and I laugh uncontrollably. He laughs at me and try to push him off me.

"Stop... stop," I gasp between laughs. He just continues to tickle me. Eventually I roll over and off the bed with a thud.

"Are you okay?" He questioned trying to stifle his laugh.

"Yeah I'm fine," I say. We settle down and start to watch a movie. I've watched at least seven movies today. Half way through it I look up. "I'm thirsty, I'll be right back." He nods at my statement.

I try to be quiet as I walk down the stairs so I don't wake anyone up. Then I hear voices. I hop off the steps and into the kitchen. Graham's parents were setting at the table fighting over something. "Gregory, I need you to tell me the truth." Mrs. Winters said firmly.

"I'm not cheating on you!" He protests. I look up to see Graham at the foot of the stairs with his index finger to his lips. He steps down to stand beside me.

"Then tell me what's going on!" She demanded.

"I-I can't yet," he says sadly. A tear runs down her cheek and he holds her hands in his. "I'm not cheating on you though. I love you, only you and nothing will ever change that."

"I love you too and nothing will change that either but I need to know," She pleads.

"You'd be surprised." He mumbled and more tears rolled.

"I need you to explain. It won't make me love you any less or change my thoughts about you." She assured and he bowed his head. Kissing her hands he looked back up into her eyes and she continued. "I saw our credit card receipt," she sniffled.

"Bethany, it's not-" he was cut off by her again.

"You've bought a lot of flowers. Who are you buying them for?" She states, her voice growing stronger. He shakes his head. "You lied to me and your children. You don't go out with your friends every weekend. So you're going someplace else. You've bought all these flowers from the florist." Then she starts to name them off. I was too consumed in their argument to realize what was right in front of me, until now. "Roses, daisies, and carnations. Over one-hundred."

He was the one putting all those flowers on my moms grave. I hadn't realized it until now. How could I be so stupid? I should have known from the first time she said flowers! My face obviously had a shocked expression. How could it not? Graham was nudging me with his elbow but I wasn't paying attention to him. "It was you," I spoke loudly and both their heads snapped to me and Graham.

"How much of that did you hear, sweetie?" Mrs. Winters asked wiping off her eyes.

"Enough to know that he's the one putting the flowers on my moms grave." I said my eyes never leaving Mr. Winters. Every eye in the room was on him and he looked guilty as hell. "How did you know my mom?"

"I didn't know her personally," he stated. "I didn't know her at all really."

"Then why all the flowers?" I interrogated.

"I didn't know she was your mother. I would have told you sooner. I was just scared-" this time it was Graham who cut him off.

"Cut to the chase, dad." He snapped, pulling me to him.

"I was the one driving the truck." The moment those words left his mouth I knew. He was the one who killed my mother and the unborn baby that I was keen on protecting.

"Why?" I asked, barely a whisper. My eyes glaze over at the thought. As do his. I just can't believe it. He was so nice to me when he met me. Why did he put flowers on my moms grave? "I want the whole story!"

Graham was rubbing my shoulders and Mrs. Winters was looking frantically from me to her husband and back again. "After work my friend and I went out for a drink. I was completely slammed when Jimmy suggested we do something crazy. I said we should steal a car and he was all for the idea. We walked, well more like staggered to a house that was about fifteen minutes away from the bar we were at. There was a really nice truck and the keys were still in the vehicle so we took it. He said we would drive it around for a bit then bring it back." He looked down at the table where his hands were, narrowing his eyes.

"But you didn't get the chance to," I elaborated and he shook his head.

"We drove around for a while. I will say that the beer bottles and cans in the truck were not ours. Otherwise it would have had our DNA. Anyways, I started to swerve as we drove and I nearly passed out. I saw headlights and tried to move out of the way. Jimmy was yelling for me to stop. Then the collision happened before I could even react. I don't remember much after that. I remember Jimmy freaking out about finger prints and wiping everything down. I had a couple cuts a scrapes but nothing major. Jimmy's head was cut and there was blood. I remember seeing the car and how bad it was. I wanted to go back, to see if you were okay but Jimmy wouldn't let me. He said you were probably dead. So we left. A week later, I saw the crash on the news. I found out that you were in the car and you lived but your mom and the baby died. I didn't know your names or what you looked like. As soon as I found out the name of your mother. I visited her grave one day out of every other weekend. I gave her flowers and then you came. I knew who you were when you said your mom had died. Then, I saw you at the grave yard. You were talking about your friends and my son and how much you wished she was there. I felt so guilty before and that made it worse. I want to make it up but I can't and I can't take it back. I was going to confess but I got scared. I didn't want to loose my family." He confessed as a tear slid down his cheek.

Anger boiled within me. "Yet you took away mine. You killed my mom and my sibling who wasn't even born!" I screamed as the tears rolled down my cheeks.

"Calm down," Graham said to me and I moved away from his touch. He looked sad at first but then he glanced at his dad and he just looked confused.

"I just found out that your dad killed my mom and you want me to calm down? I wanted to know who killed her and now I do." I said to them, Mr. Winters looked guilty as he should.

"He's still my dad Reese. Besides he said he felt bad and it was an accident." Graham tried but all I felt was a jab to my heart.

"This is not like accidentally poured juice on me! He murdered my mom. My dad left. So I was stuck with Jay. I'm sure you can imagine what that was like." I spat bitterly.

His eyes grew angry and his features tensed. "My father is not a murderer." He denied but his dad put a hand in his shoulder.

"Yes I am," he whispered and I backed up.

"It was an accident. He didn't mean to." He said more to himself than me.

"He killed my mom! That's murder!"I exasperated.

"Maybe it was meant to happen. Maybe you were meant to get stuck with Jay. I'm starting to think you deserve it." Graham snapped and I felt my heart shatter instantly.

"Maybe I do," I whispered. I ran upstairs and grabbed my bag. When I got down stairs I saw Mrs. Winters hugging her husband tightly, sobbing and Graham siting at the table rubbing his temples. He looked up and saw me.

"I'm sorry, Reese. You didn't deserve what I said and you definitely don't deserve what he does to you. I was just mad and trying to defend my father and was completely out of line." He apologized to me with a look of sorrow. It morphed to one of pure panic when he saw my bag. I turned on my heel and walked out of the house with a pleading Graham behind me. "No, please don't leave!" he grabbed my hand but I ripped it away from him. "Don't go back there! Don't leave me!" He begged.

"Get off, I deserve it remember?" I ask bitterly like the bitch I am. He tried to pull me into a hug but I lurched away from him. I don't think he'll hurt me. He said he cared. Even though I'm having a hard time believing that now. I still don't think he'll hurt me. It was just a reflex.

I couldn't take the hurt look on his face, so I turned around. "What have I done?" He whispered to himself. I walked for a minute and I didn't hear foot steps behind me anymore.

I know now. I know who killed her. It wasn't in cold blood like I had originally thought. It was an accident but I can't forgive him. He may feel guilty but he should. I hope the guilt eats him alive. Graham told me I deserve the hits and I believe him but it just hurt. I thought he liked me but it's obvious he doesn't.

I reach my house and step inside, slamming the door. I'm just looking for trouble tonight. "Stop slamming stuff! I'm hungry!" Jay yells from the living room. I stomp off to the kitchen and throw pots and pans around making a ton of noise. He angrily walked into the kitchen and slaps me. "I told you to stop slamming things around!"

"Sorry, I'm just angry." I sighed and he rolled his eyes.

"About what?" He asked and I looked up with hopeful eyes. Maybe he cares, he might love me like I've wished for him to. He might want to adopt me.

"I found out who killed my mom." I stated and that oddly enraged him. He grabbed me by the throat his eyes growing dark. "Don't you want to know?" I struggled to get out.

"No! I don't want to hear about your whore of a mother. Her baby probably wasn't even mine." He yelled and I felt a surge of anger go through me.

"Really, because you raped her every chance you got!" I shouted back, causing his grip on my throat to tighten. I wasn't going to back down though. I must be suicidal. "If she would have even been seen with another man you would have been the one to kill her." This must be how Graham felt. If it were the other way around I would stand up for my mom, but he said I deserve it.

He threw me into the floor and started to kick my stomach. He kicked and kicked until I was coughing up blood. "Don't speak like that to me again, or I'll make it worse for you." He threatened me. Worse beatings? I think I'll tone it down. I don't want anymore scars.

I crawled down the stairs with my bag and laid on the floor with blood still coming out if my mouth. I coughed and coughed, more blood falling from my mouth after each one. I managed to pick myself up, with my bag in hand I left the house. I was going to Adrienne's she would be there for me whenever I needed her. I could count on her.

I reach her house and knock on the door. She opens the door with sleepiness clouding her face. She sees me and get eyes widen in shock. "Oh my gosh!"

"He-" I try but start to cough again, sputtering blood on my hands again.

She quieted me and pulled me in the house. "Your okay, we need to call someone and get you to the hospital." I shook my head violently at her suggestion. Then the idea struck me. I pulled out my phone and pressed call on Andy's contact.

"Hello?" He answered and I tried to speak.

"Andy-" more blood sputtering coughs.

"Reese? Are you okay? Where are you?" He rambles sounding tense. I put the phone on speaker and Adrienne helped me.

"We have a situation." Ad spoke for me.

"Is she okay?" He asked and she replied with a no. "Does she need medical attention?" He questioned and shook my head rapidly.

"No," she sighed. "Just come here!" With that she gave Andy her address and he was there within minutes. He burst through the door.

"Where is she? Is she okay?" As soon as he sees me he is by my side looking me over. "There's blood in your lips."

I pulled my shirt up to expose the bruised skin on my stomach. "I was walking around and I was jumped." I lied and he have me a look. He knows in lying.

"Twice in three weeks, huh?" He asks tilting his head. "Seems highly unlikely. Just admit that your step dad is abusing you." He exasperated the last sentence.

Maybe if I tell him things will get better. "I'm not abused," I deny. It's just punishment. He shakes his head and looks at my stomach. I pull my shirt back down.

"You need to go to the hospital. I think one of your ribs are cracked. You're stomach is completely bruised and from the looks of it you were coughing up blood." Andy analyzed me with a look of pity. I hate pity.

"I'm fine, I don't need to go to the hospital." He scoffs at my response.

"Come on let me drive you to the hospital. They'll set your ribs and you'll be good to go. Also they can help with that cut." He offered, motioning to the cut on my side from the knife Jay had used on me a while back.

"Fine," I sigh. Both Adrienne and Andy get a little excited but Andy covers it up quickly.

"Let's go," he takes my hand and helps me out of the house and into the car. Adrienne decided to go with us and then let me stay with her tonight.

Chapter 23

Once I got to the hospital, I found out that one of my ribs were cracked and the cut from before needed stitches. They gave me pain medication and some bandages. Andy drove us back to Adrienne's house and we went to sleep after she forced me to take the medication. I can handle the pain. I mean, yes it hurts but I've taken it this long. I think I can handle a little while longer. Besides, I've had worse.

In the morning, Adrienne decided to wake me up. "Reese," she yelled into my ear.

"What?" I asked softly setting up from my place on the floor. "What time is it?"

"Five," she replies simply.

"You let me sleep until five?" I asked in bewilderment. She laughed a little and I noticed the darkness in the room. There was no way the sun had set already.

"It's five in the morning." She notified with a chuckle. I glared in her direction and she just laughed.

"Why would you commit such a sin?" I asked playfully. She tugged me out of bed in a fit of giggles and down the stairs. She made breakfast. Too bad she decided to do that now and not at ten. "What's all this for?"

There was a large stack of pancakes. Knowing I love tea, there was a big pitcher of it. Butter and syrup were towards the middle and there was a plate of bacon beside them. "This is my apology breakfast." She said lowering her head.

"Why would you need to apologize?" I asked, completely confused. She sighed sitting down at the table.

"I didn't even notice your bruises." She looked so upset.

"Yes you did, I showed you and you said I needed to go to the hospital." I defended shaking my head slightly at her.

"You were being abused and I didn't notice. I was never there for you and then last night that happened." She pointed to my stomach.

"Where were you last night?" I asked and she just smiled, already knowing what I'm getting at. "You were with me because I needed you. You were there for me. You're one of my best friends. I know I can count on you and Cameron for anything. I'm sorry that I didn't tell you until now but I was afraid." I explained and she looked confused and overjoyed.

"Afraid of what?" She asked tilting her head.

"Afraid that if he found out I told anyone he would hurt me more. Afraid that if I told you," I paused and looked up at her. "You would think less of me," I admitted.

She brought me in for a hug. "I could never think any less of you. You are so brave it's actually kind of ridiculous sometimes." She said making both of us laugh. "Now we need to eat."

We ate over half of the pancake stack, drank all the tea, and saved most of the bacon for Cameron since we both know he will be over later. "We have school today, don't we?" I question Adrienne.

She gives me a look of dread as we clean up the kitchen. I clean up the counter while she washed the dishes. "We should get ready."

After we take our showers and what not, we get our bags and walk to school. Once we arrive at school I see Graham standing at the door. Just standing there. Bags under his eyes and he looks like he hasn't slept in days. Worry and stress were etched on his face as he scanned the crowd of people going to enter the building.

When he saw me he tried to make his way over to me. He pushed through the people and finally he was standing in front of me. "We need to talk," he breathed. I nodded to Adrienne, telling her to go into the school. She walks away and Graham sighs. Eventually, the school entrance was empty except for Graham and I. "I'm sorry, let me explain." He exasperated.

"Explain what? Why you think I deserve to be hit? I know I do but just for a minute you had me convinced I didn't. I was wrong though. I do deserve it, you're right." I almost yelled. I turned in my heel and started to walk the opposite direction of the school. He followed closely behind me.

"I didn't mean it. I was just really mad and you insulted my dad. I was just standing up for him. I'm so sorry," he rapidly tried to explain himself and walked behind me. He was jogging beside me now. It shouldn't be this hard to keep up with me. I mean, I'm kinda a little beat up.

I knew what it was like though. I knew how it felt to want to stand up for someone you love. It's hard to keep your mouth shut. I guess I couldn't be mad. I was just hurt. "I know, but I also know you meant it." I added then slowed my pace a little as it hurt to much to keep going.

"I didn't mean it, I swear to you. I was just mad." He tried yet again and I shook my head.

"You were so mad that you lied?" I asked turning to him. "You had to lie to me and hurt my feelings just because I made you mad. I would never to that to you. I may say some mean things in defense to my mom or dad but I wouldn't beat you down unless whatever I'm saying is true." With that I turned to walk again and he caught up with me easily.

"I know what I did was wrong and I won't do it again. I just felt like I had to stand up for him! I didn't think about what you were feeling at the time. Please just think about it for a minute." He sighed and I kept walking.

He was right. Also, he was telling the truth. I could tell. I liked him and I think I was falling in love with him. No I knew I loved him. I had let him in and this is what happened. I've learned that if you fall in love with someone, their harsh words only seem more harsh. It really matters what they think of you.

I had fallen in love with Graham Winters. I forgave him already I just didn't know what to say. All these feelings of guilt, anger, hurt, and overwhelming feelings of bliss and love hit me at once. All I wanted to do was cry.

My eyes started to water and I glanced at Graham and saw him battling with himself in his head over something. I didn't want him to see me so weak. So I quickened my pace and started to jog away as he stood still. "Reese," he said with a small voice. It seemed like he was trying to say something but the words wouldn't come out. I kept walking. He was getting irritated but I wouldn't stop. Then I heard something that made me pull myself to an abrupt halt. "Dammit, Reese. I love you!" He shouts.

I was too stunned to say anything. I never thought that someone like him could love someone like me. Here he is saying that he does love me when I was just admitting to myself that I loved him. Now I wonder if I have the guts to tell him.

"I love you, and you don't give up on someone you love. So I'll stay here all day and night if I have to." He demands sternly as he walks up to me.

Should I tell him? What will he do? Here goes nothing. "I love you too," my voice was so soft and quiet that if he wasn't as close as he is he wouldn't have heard it. A large smile broke out on his face and he picked me up and spun me around. I giggled and he set me on my feet.

"I would like to take you on a date Ms. Fode," he insisted and I smiled up at him.

Wrapping my arms around him I mumbled, "I can't wait." He embraced me tightly, gently kissing my head.

I wanted a relationship with Graham. I wanted to be happy for once. The only time I was happy before was when I was with Adrienne or Cameron. Now I have Graham to make me happy too. I'm turning 18 soon so I should be getting out of the Jay situation. Maybe I could get emancipated?

Now is the thing I need to be thinking about. Graham's father, or Gregory. He has been put through hell and trust me I know what that feels like. He killed my mom but it was an accident. A terrible mistake. I can't forgive him, at least not anytime soon, but I should give it a shot. He obviously felt guilty and it seemed like it was eating him alive. I knew that he would be jeopardizing his family but he has to confess. I know what it's like to lose someone you love. It sucks but he can come back. My mom can't. He can get out of jail because I'm not going to press charges. I don't know how long it will take but he'll be back with his family. Now I just have to talk to him. "Graham, I want to talk to your dad."

He looked hesitant. "I don't think that's-" he started but I cut him off.

"I'm calm and I've sorted everything out." I tried to convince him and it seemed to have worked. He sighed, nodding. We went back to school and then I went home with Graham. I was nervous to talk to his father but it had to be done.

Once Graham's father arrived Graham instantly stiffened. I kissed his cheek knowing where this was going. I sat down at the kitchen table and waited for him to come into his kitchen. Graham sat beside me, looking more nervous than me.

Gregory saw me and guilt flooded his face. "What are you doing here?" He asked me.

"I want to talk." I explained and he sat down at the table.

"Okay?" He said, sounding more like a question.

I sighed and began. "What you did was probably the biggest mistake ever. I don't know if I can forgive you." Graham's head dropped thinking he knew where I was going with this. "But I'll try my best to." Graham's head shot up in shock. Gregory looked utterly confused but relieved.

"But why?" He asked and I smile sadly.

"You took my mom away from me and you just left us there." Yes I was trying to make his feel bad. Don't judge me. "That was a mistake but people make mistakes all the time. This stuff happens all the time. Not many people feel remorse though. You felt guilty and you tried to make it up the best you could without losing your family." I explained, he looked at me only blinking. Where as Graham was looking at me with pure amazement. Maybe even adoration.

"Thank you," Gregory mumbled.

"I'll try to forgive you." I hesitated before continuing, " I want you to confess."

To my surprise he smiled at me. "I was going to. I wanted to do it in the morning. So I could have one last night with my family." It was more like he was asking me if it was okay. I smiled and nodded. I can't believe he was going to confess. I felt a weight lift off my shoulders as he said that.

"I'll leave and you can spend time with your family." I stood up and went to leave when a hand grabbed my wrist. I turned to see Mr. Winters as he pulled me into a hug. I tensed at first but then I returned the hug.

"I'm so sorry, Reese. Thank you for being so kind after everything I've put you through." He let go of me with a smile and Graham walked me over to the door.

Once we reached the door Graham grabbed my hand. "That was definitely not what I was expecting." He admitted to me, while he rubbed his thumb over my knuckles. "I'm not excited that he's confessing but it's what needs to be done. I'm sorry that this is happening."

I smiled half-heartedly at him as he pulled me to his chest. "I better go, go spend time with your dad." I said into his chest. He hugged me tighter and kissed the top of my head.

"Goodbye, I'll see you tomorrow." He said and I walked down his driveway and onto the road. He watched me until I was almost halfway down the road then he went back into his house.

Once I reach home Jay is setting at the kitchen table with an empty plate. He saw me and his lip turned into a sneer. "I've been sitting here for half an hour waiting for my food. I get home from a hard day of work and no ones home to make me dinner!" He yells, slamming his fist down on the table. He never comes home this early anyways!

He kept on yelling and shouting profanities at me but I decided to block them out as I made some lasagna. I sat down at the kitchen table waiting for the food to bake. He just continued to put me down for an hour. Telling me how much of a disgrace I was.

Eventually, I heard the ding and stood up to get the food. He then sat down and took a break from his screaming.

I took his plate and dished out the lasagna. Then, did the same for myself. I gave him a lot more than I gave myself. Once I sat down he gave me a look of disgust. "Are you really going to eat all that?"

I looked down at my food and pushed the plate away. "No, I'm not hungry." I lied, I'm pretty hungry but he's right. That's too much food. I put my untouched lasagna back into the pan and the dish in the sink as start walking off to the basement.

"Good, you could lose some weight." He added before I was out of hearing range. I sighed and turned on the television after I plop onto the couch.

Chiller sounds good. A movie called Below Zero came on so I decided to watch it. I had to rewind it and watch it twice to understand it. I was confused the first time. Soon, I drifted off to sleep.

After getting ready in the morning I headed off to school. Once I arrived I saw Graham waiting for me outside, in the parking lot. I ran to him with a small smile on my face and he hugged me tight. Wrapping an arm around my waist, he lead me to the entrance of the school. "How was it this morning?" I asked and looked down. I felt guilty.

I didn't want to take his dad away from him. I just wanted justice for my mom. "He confessed and they took him into custody. It wasn't all that bad. They want to see you as well." He notified and I looked up at him in confusion.

"Why?" I asked, tilting my head to the side.

"To ask you about pressing charges and thing like that." Graham said as his body stiffened.

I smiled slightly, "I'm not pressing charges. Your dad will only spend as much time as he has to. I'm going to try and make it as short as possible." I assured him and he relaxed with a smile as he kissed my cheek. The bell sounded and we walked to class.

At the end of the day, Graham stopped me before I could leave. I was standing by my locker when he called out to me. "Reese," I turn to him as he approaches me. "Do you want to go on that date Friday?" He asked looking a little nervous.

"Sure sounds great," I replied. I'm surprised that he is so upbeat. I mean, his father is in custody and is going to end up in prison yet he seems oddly happy. I know that I would be down in the dumps if it were reversed. I would ask but it just doesn't seem like the right thing to do.

"I'll pick you up around seven?" He suggested and I nodded with a smile. He kissed my cheek and jogged up to Nick with a smile. I walked home and started to make dinner.

I decided on steak and mashed potatoes. As hungry as I was I didn't eat. Jay was right, I needed to lose some weight. I went into the basement and then to my art room. I haven't been working on any art lately. I love art. It's kind of like a release for me.

I pull out some clay and sculpting tools. Place plastic over the table and get started on the sculpt. I never really know what I'm going to do before I start it. I just go with whatever pops into my head as I continue or I just work with what I've already done. Sometimes I give myself a topic and then I work from there.

After five hours I have a sculpt. It's a face, but it's not a human face. It's some being, I haven't decided what it is yet. It's got spikes all over it's head and face. However, there is none around the nose area. Even though it doesn't have a nose. It's lips have small spikes along with the chin and the neck. It's head has large spikes that are directed backwards. There was no eyebrows and no ears. The farther out the face got, the longer the spikes. I took my paint and my new air brush and started to color it. I made it blue and black.

The main color was a midnight blue color. That spikes faded into a deep black. On the lips and other small spikes they were completely black. I painted the eyes black. After I finished with the paint I set it up on a shelf to dry. I cleaned all the clay and paint up. Then I washed my hands and arms in the bathroom.

Now I'm ready for bed. I change into pajamas and lay down, waiting for sleep to come to me.

Chapter 24

The week went by fast and I had already answered all the questions the police had for me. I didn't press any charges and they said he wouldn't get more than twenty years at the most. The court date was set for next month.

Before I knew it I was calling Adrienne to ask her to help me get ready for the date. "Hey, I need your help." I asked her and she seemed a little worried at first.

"Do you need a place to stay or something?" She asked me and I laughed.

"No, I have a date." The second those words left my mouth I heard a high pitch squeal.

"Graham finally asked you out?" She screeched in my ear. She sounded like she was hyperventilating over the line.

"Yes and this is my first date ever so I don't know what to wear or anything." I began to panic and I went on.

"I'll be right over just have everything out and ready for me." She demanded and I smiled and my best friends enthusiasm of the situation.

"Make sure to be quiet and come in the back door." I reminded her and she replied with a simple "okay" before hanging up. I ran to get everything while she was on her way.

I grabbed some makeup such as mascara, eyeliner, and eyeshadow. Then I moved on to outfits. I picked out some of my favorite shirts and some more classy shirts along with jeans. Shortly I heard a car pull in my drive way. I knew it was Adrienne because Jay was at some hotel and wouldn't be home until midnight, maybe later.

She came and knocked to which I opened the door. She squealed again and pulled me onto the couch. She applied some light brown eyeshadow and bold eyeliner along with light mascara. She looked at all my clothes I had laid out and she chose some dark washed skinny jeans and stylish black and white shirt. I don't even remember laying that out. It was loose and most of it was black with white swirls around the neck that was low cut. Just enough to show off some cleavage.

"No," I said as she held up the shirt. I didn't want my boobs showing. She gave me a pout and I gave in. I went into the bathroom and changed then came out where she was holding up a pair of combat boots. I smiled excitedly and slipped them on. Then she straightened my hair and told me not to mess anything up until he got here.

"You better call me with details," she threatened.

"Absolutely," I hugged her and she left to go home.

I watched some television until I heard a knock on the side door. I stood up and opened the door with a smile. Graham stood there for a minute just checking me out. I suddenly felt self-conscious about my appearance. I turned around to get my phone and money then we left.

"Where are we going?" I asked and he shot me a smile that would have made my knees weak and cause me to fall. Good thing we were in the car and I was sitting down.

"I'm not telling," he smirks at me then his smirk drops and he starts to look nervous. "You l-look very beautiful." I blush and look away. That seems to send him into a panic state. "Not that you don't normally look beautiful. You always look beautiful. I was just saying-"

"Thank you, Graham. You look very handsome yourself." I cut off his cute rambling. His hair was styled to perfection. He was wearing a grey button-up shirt and a black hoodie over it. Along with jeans and black Jordan's.

He laughed and looked back at the road, mumbling a thanks. Soon we pulled up in a small parking lot. I looked at the sign and began to laugh. He looked at me and smiled. "What?" He asked.

"Glow in the dark mini-golf is not one of my best sports," I admit. He just shrugs smiling even wider.

"Me either," he says as he takes my hand in his and kisses my knuckles.

*************************(Graham's POV)

I can't even think straight. She just looks so beautiful. More than usual, maybe it's just the lighting. Or maybe it's just her. She blushes as I kiss her hand. I'm glad that I have this effect on her.

I pull her up to the counter where a girl that looks our age with long blonde hair and freckles greets us. She bats her eyes flirtatiously at me and I can feel Reese tense beside me. I hand the girl the money as she gives me a card with everything we need on it. I kiss Reese on the cheek to let the blonde chick know that I was taken.

Well I hoped to be taken soon. I'm going to ask Reese to be my girlfriend at the end of the date. I also want to kiss her. I smile down at her beautiful face. "I'm telling you, I suck at this." She says as she looks out at the course. There was one large one and a bunch of small ones.

"Come on!" I pull her out to the course and she sighs. "Ladies first," I say politely as I step aside. She laughs and takes the shot.

It goes straight into the hole and she looks up at me. It was the first hole and she had a look of doubt on her face. "Your turn," she says throwing a golf ball at me. I smile and make the shot. After about eighteen holes she starts to struggle. Getting frustrated, she swung as hard as she could at the ball. We heard a loud crash and she winced.

"I think that could be considered in the rough," I note and she scowls at me. She hit it straight throw the window of the house next to the course.

"Who would want to live next to a mini golf course anyways?" She exasperates. I laugh and she does too as we finish up the courses.

"Next stop is food," I state and she looks down. She looked like she had lost weight. I noticed but I just didn't say anything. Now I know why she's lost some weight. "When was the last time you ate?"

"Last week," she grumbles. I openly gape at her.

"You need to eat," I insist.

"I'm fat, I need to lose weight." She objects and I walk up to her. I grab her shoulders and look into her eyes.

"Who told you that?" I asked, gently. She looked down.

"Jay," she murmured. Jay? Who's Jay Wait, the step dad.

"Your step dad?" I asked her, trying to keep the anger and edge out of my voice. She nods silently. I shook my head at her. "You are not fat. You're too skinny if anything. Baby, please eat?" I pleaded and she hugged me with a slight shiver. Maybe from the name I just called her?

"Okay, where are we going to eat?" She asked and I smiled triumphantly.

"Mc Donald's," I say and she smiles. I'm glad I can help her. She takes my hand and we walk out together.

Once we arrive at the fast food restaurant, we both order bacon cheese burgers. I'm surprised that it's her favorite because it's mine too. She scarfs down the whole burger and drinks all her Pepsi. I watch her and she smiles sheepishly. Murmuring a simple "sorry".

"Don't be sorry. I'm so happy you're eating. Trust me I know how good the burger is." I say with a smile and she sends me one back. We talk and laugh the whole time then a man in his late thirties came up to us.

"I apologize but we're closing," He notified us. My eyes widened as I look at the time, it's midnight.

"We'll be on our way then," I reply as I take Reese's hand and lead her to the door. Tossing away our trash as we leave. "Did you enjoy this?" I questioned quietly, too afraid she'd say no.

"I had a blast and I can safely say it's the best date I've ever been on." She giggles.

"How many have you been on?" I ask, I know I'm jealous. I don't want other guys to go on dates with her to flirt with her. I want her to be mine.

"One, including this one." She says looking at me. Yes!

"You've only been on one date?" I asked, shocked. I couldn't keep the smile off my face as I said that. She nodded and I smiled even wider. "I'm happy that I was your first. Can I look forward to being your second too?" I add with a hopeful look.

She giggles again. How I love her laugh. "Yes," she said and I start the engine of my car. I want to be the only guy she ever goes on dates with.

Suddenly, my phone rings. I see that it's my sister. "Hello?" I answer. Reese is currently looking out the window to give me my privacy as best she can. Considering the call is coming through my radio I don't think she can just not listen.

"I need you to pick me up from Nicks house." Brianna states, no, more like demands.

"Why are you at Nicks house?" I ask angrily. You see, Brianna and Nick were officially dating now. So who knows what they were up to.

"There was a party. I need a ride home so come get me." She said and I was officially pissed.

"Whatever, I'll be there in twenty minutes." I agree and hang up. "I'mso sorry that I have to pick up my sister." I say to Reese.

"It's cool, I can just walk home from here." She says as she tries to open the door but I lock it. She turns to me with a look of confusion.

"You're not walking home alone on our date. You're not walking home alone at all. I just have to stop and get her then I can take you home and walk you to your door. Then I have to yell at her for interrupting my date." I reason and she laughs shaking her head.

I drive until I see Nick's house. Lights were flashing and music was blaring. My sister stood out on the lawn with Holly by her side. Oh, hell no!

"You said you, not her." I said threateningly to Brianna and she just shrugged as they both hopped in the back seat. I sighed giving Reese a look and she smiled grabbing my hand.

"Were we interrupting something?" Holly sneered.

"Ye-" I started to tell off the bitch but Reese squeezed my hand tightly and gave me a pleading look. I turned back to the road and drove Reese home.

Once we were there she looked at me and I got out with her to walk her to her door, like I said I would. "Thank you for tonight. It was amazing!" She said earnestly.

"I thought so too. I was wondering if you wanted to be my girlfriend?" I asked nervously and all at once.

She was silent for a moment and I began to panic. What if she says no? "I would love to be your girlfriend, Graham." She said with the biggest smile I've ever seen her wear.

Now, I'm ready. I slowly leaned in and placed my hand on her cheek. I brought her face close to mine, brushing our lips as if to ask if it was okay. She took a step forward and I went to do it. To finally kiss her but you know way happened?

HONK! HONK! The horn of the car sounded and I pulled away from Reese to see Holly with a glare towards us ushering me to come over so we can leave. Every time!

"This is getting ridiculous." I say to Reese as I look at her I see something cross her eyes. I was going to ask what was wrong but before I could the horn sounded again. "I guess I'll see you soon," I sigh and that same emotion crosses her eyes again. I went to leave.

"Graham wait!" She called out when I was half way back to the car. I turned back to her, confused. She ran up to me and hesitated for a moment.

"What's wrong?" I asked.

"Nothing's wrong I just-" she stopped and looked at her house then to me again.

"Reese wh-" that's all I got out. She sighed and put her hand on my neck, pulling my head to her. She crashed her lips to mine and I was shocked at first but responded as soon as I could. I put my hands on her back and waist as our lips moves in sync. I ran my tongue across her bottom lip and she parted her lips slightly. I shot my tongue into her mouth, exploring every inch. Then she pulled back to get some air.

"Sorry," she said breathlessly. She was flushed and looking everywhere but me.

I took my hand and put it on her cheek so she would look in my eyes. "Do you know how long I've been waiting for that kiss?" I asked her and we both laughed. "I have to go. I'll talk to you soon, girlfriend." I said with a smirk as I gently kissed her lips. She then retreated to her house as I got into the car. Wow! It was definitely worth the wait. I think I just fell harder for this girl.

(Reese's POV)

I don't know what came over me. I just really wanted to kiss him, so I did. It was the best feeling ever! Our lips moved perfectly together and it was like fireworks were going off. It was amazing. I think I'm falling harder for this boy.

I heard a slam coming from upstairs and I knew Jay was home. He probably saw the kiss as well. I'm so screwed. I sat down on the couch, not wanting to go upstairs. I pulled out the sketching pad my mom had got me when I was sixteen. Taking one of my black colored pencils, I began to draw. Eventually, the small black lines and marks had become a drawing. A drawing of Graham. He was standing shirtless with a heart on his hand.

You may be thinking of a different heart, the kind that children draw on their papers at school or something. No, this is an actual heart. The organ inside someone's chest. It may be weird but it had a meaning. Graham held my heart in his hands. I loved him and that's what is supposed to be shown in this picture. The shirtlessness is just for me. His chiseled abs are very defined and his jaw is sharp. I tried to make his face as real as I could. To be honest it looked pretty good.

Throughout the whole time I was drawing and putting my stuff away, there was continuous loud banging upstairs. I changed my close. Slipping into some tight black shorts and a Pierce the Veil band shirt. Not finding time to take off my makeup before my name was shouted. "Reese!" Jays voice boomed through the house.

I sighed as I headed up the stairs. I know my makeup was still on and that would make him angry. I slowly walk into the kitchen. I'm shocked by the mess. There is shattered glass, pots, and pans scattered all over the floor. I step in and around the broken glass, seeing as I'm barefoot. "What did you do in here?" I asked. I knew he would make me clean it all up.

"Who was that boy you were kissing?" He growls dangerously. "Scratch that, you were shoving your tongue down his throat." I kept quiet as he approached me.

 I just don't understand why he would care what I was doing. So I asked, "Why do you care?"

"Who was he?" He avoids my question.

"His name is Graham." I answer and he seems to only get more angry.

"You're not allowed to have a boyfriend. You're not allowed to kiss anyone. Your-" he stops himself short with a wide smirk covering his lips. "You think he likes you. No one can ever like you. You will never be wanted." He lets me know.

"I don't think he likes me." I start and he smirks ever wider but his smirk fades quickly when I say my next sentence. "I think he loves me."

His fist connects with the wall beside my head. He rips it out and I check out the damage. He left a large gash in the wall. "Clean this up!" He yells and that's when I snap.

I'm so sick of having to clean all this up. I'm tired of cooking all the time and I'm done with being bossed around so easily. "No," I say with my newly found confidence. He looks irate but it doesn't faze me quiet yet.

"You will obey me!" He slaps me across the face and it just pisses me off. I push him back off me and stomp into the living room. When I pushed him it was enough to startle him and take a few steps back. I'm not that strong. He soon follows me into the living room. He doesn't look too mad more like shocked. I guess this is the first time I've ever stood up for myself. "Come with me," he steps towards the door.

"Where are we going?" I asked suspiciously. He gives me a hard glare and grabs my arm to try and yank me out the front door. "No!" I yell, shoving myself away from him, Only to fall on the floor. He bends down with both arms and grips me roughly. I thrash, kick, and scream from underneath him. I see him reaching for something with his right hand.

He drew his arm back and hit me in the head with what I assume is vase or something. I know it was glass and it had shattered as it hit me. Pain shot throughout my head and I felt hot liquid running down my face and neck. My vision began to blur and all Jay became was a blob of color. Soon after, everything went black.

Chapter 25

As I crack my eyes open, everything is blurry. Suddenly, a bright light hit my eyes making me close them and groan lightly. When I open them again my eyes adjust. I was laying down in the back seat of Jay's truck. I sat up and looked out of the wind-shield. I almost laid back down as I became dizzy and light-headed.

"Where are we going?" I asked rubbing my eyes. As I looked into the rear-view mirror I noticed the reddish brown color in my hair and on my face and neck. It was dried blood. There was a slow and painful pounding in my head and I saw a gash on the left side of my face beside my hair line, moving back into my brown hair.

I press my fingers to it and hiss at the pain it caused. He glance up at me before going back to the road. "We're almost there just shut up!" He snaps obviously angry. I decide to keep my mouth shut. I had already made him mad enough to smash some glass over my head.

I just sat there, looking out the window as we passed trees and very few cars. Throughout the past ten minutes I've only seen one car. He slowly pulls up to a small parking lot. Outside of a park.

Confusion filled me. He stepped out of the vehicle and I followed. "Why are we here?" I asked and he avoided my question.

Shoving me I front of him, he spoke. "Go!" I walked around aimlessly. Every time I would wonder off in the wrong direction he would push me back on track. Soon we came to a trail that went through a large patch of woods. He nudged me roughly into it and I followed it's seemingly endless twists and turns. Eventually there was a small clearing. A little bigger than the parking lot. I remember this place. It's the cliff. It's towards the end of the rail road tracks, about twenty minutes away. At the bottom of the cliff there was a raging storm of water crashing against rocks. Wait, why am I here?

"What's going on?" I asked as I looked back to Jay, who stood at the tree line. He smirked maliciously at me. Taking a step closer, then another. He stood before me with his arms crossed over his chest.

"You remind me so much of your mother. Which is why you disgust me. You're even worse." My heart dropped to my stomach as the words fell from his lips.

There was still a little hope left. I mean he cried when she died. "Well, you married her." I noted aloud, he glared at me. He slowly took more steps towards me, causing me to back up.

"Yes, I loved her. However, I don't love you. I hate you. You are disgusting and weak and worthless. Your own mother didn't want you but she kept you because your father didn't want you either. He left and she was stuck with you. She used to complain about you to me all the time. When you turned five you both moved in and that's when I realized why she didn't want you. You barely ever talked but when you did you wanted something. You always complained about everything. She had to pay for a monster! She bought you all kinds of stuff and you were never grateful. You always wanted more." He told me and I started to believe him.

My mom did buy me things sometimes if I asked, but I always said thank you. I tried to be polite. I don't really remember much about my childhood. I remember that I was five when he started to hit me, that's about it. I believed him. I was a monster, but maybe he was lying. Either way I'm different now. "Why did you bring me here?" I asked him and he smirked again.

"Because I hate you. My life has been miserable ever since you came into it. I want you gone. Remember when I said that I was happy you'd be gone in a while?" He asked and I recalled him saying that to me. I was going to be eighteen so I'd leave.

"Yes," I replied weakly.

"Well this is what I meant." He ground out darkly. He reached his hand behind his back and pulled out a silver gun, pointing it at my head. I took a step back and gasped as I almost fell off the cliff. He had me cornered and if I took a step back I'd fall to my death, if I moved any other way he'd shoot me.

I looked back up at him fear clear in my expression as my eyes glass over. His features are angry and his grip on the gun is tight. I'm going to die tonight.

(Officer Andy's POV)

As I was driving to Reese's house to take to her about Mr. Winters, I couldn't help but worry about her. She was most likely alone with that step father of hers. He was in the middle of an adoption. He signed the papers and sent them in now he's just waiting on feed back.

I don't know why he's adopting her anyways. He treats her like crap and she just lets him. She probably thinks that I know about the abuse, and she's right because I do. I hate the fact that I can't help her. She has to openly tell me and she won't.

I've grown very attached to this girl and I haven't know her very long. She's so sweet and she's being hurt. She needs to stand up for herself but I already know she's scared. She's too scared to tell anyone. She probably thinks he'll hurt her more or maybe she thinks he loves her. I want to help her.

I pull up to her house and notice that the lights are on, but there are no cars. Confused, I walk up to the door and knock. No answer. I glance in the window of the house and notice a circle of red on the carpet. I step in front of the window to take a better look. It's a red puddle on the floor of the living room. I'm almost positive it's blood. Which gives me a reason to enter without a warrant. I open the door easily, seeing as it's unlocked.

As I step inside I keep my hand on my holster so I can have access to my gun as quick as possible if something goes wrong. I walk over to the red spot and confirm that it's blood. I hastily walk around the house. The kitchen was a mess and there was beer bottles and cans everywhere. Even some empty vodka bottles by the television. I looked at the steps and cautiously went up them. As I reached the top I saw three rooms I opened the door to one and it was like a storage room.

I began to wonder if she was hurt or dead and her body was in here. I brushed off that thought and shut the door behind me. I went to the next door on the other side of the stair case and opened it. There was a faint stench and it looked like a closet. Almost immediately after I noticed the smell, I noticed something else. There was blood all over the door of the closet and it looked like bloody handprints along with marks and scratches in the wood.

My heart hurt at seeing this. Poor Reese. I close the door silently and walk to the last one, opening it slowly and peeking my head in. I knew they weren't here but I still wanted to be careful.

It was a bed room. There was a large bed in the middle of the room and a desk against the wall beside the door. It had a desk lamp and a couple papers and pencils. I went through the drawers and the second one I opened had a notebook in it. I decided to go through it and it seemed to be a journal. It had messy cursive hand writing.

As I read it I realized it was Reese's step fathers journal. Why does he have a journal?

February 13, 2011.

I'm being forced into therapy. Apparently, there is something different going on with my head. I over-heard them talking to Madeline and my mom. They said I was crazy to sum it up. They also said I should keep a journal to vent my "feelings" too. It would help with my anger.

I flipped through almost half the book and started to read again.

April 28, 2014.

She's dead, I can't believe she's dead. That bitch left me, not only that but she left me with her terrible excuse for a daughter. I hate this girl, more than I've ever hated anyone. I don't know what it is about her. She just gets on my nerves. I can't live with her any longer. Even if it's just for a year. I have to get rid of her. I have a plan.

As I flipped through the rest of the pages, I realized that the entries weren't like the others. They were more scribbled and frantic. It was his plan. There were different possibilities of how, when, and where he would kill her. It looks like he was battling with himself, trying to find the most efficient plan.

He decided on trying to make it look like a suicide. He would take her to the cliff in the next town over, shoot her and have her fall over the cliff, tossing the gun down after. He thinks it's a perfect plan and he put a lot into this. However, there are faults.

There will be gun powder residue on his hands and not hers. So if they want to check him, realizing it's not a suicide, they will find the residue on his hands. As long as they tried to test him within the first couple days.

I looked at the date he was going to kill her. It's today. I dashed out of the house and into the car, taking the journal with me. I'm going to save her. I just hope it's not too late.

It's about forty-five minutes away. I can do this. I was pushing the speed limit a bit. I pulled into the parking lot of the area. I saw Reese's step fathers truck and I searched it. Neither of them were anywhere to be found. I took off in the direction of the cliff.

Hold on Reese.

(Reese's POV)

"Just put the gun down, I'll leave and I won't come back." I try to convince him he was absolutely enraged. He's been telling me why he hates me and how I was a disgusting whore. The usual. Then he told me how he was going to kill me.

"No!" He yelled making me flinch. "The only way to be sure that you're gone is to kill you myself. You'll be gone and I can be happy again!"

"Don't do this. It's murder, you'll go to prison. You won't be happy there." I told him watching his facial expressions and actions warily.

"I have to. I want to." He admits and tears fall down my face. I might as well except it. I'm going to die anyways.

"Okay," is all I said he gave me a look of confusion before I closed my eyes and stood there waiting.

I listen but nothing came. Suddenly, I heard a voice. "Freeze!" My eyes shot open. It was Andy! I have never been so happy to see him! He was going to save me!

"Oh," Jay sneered. "Are you sleeping with him too?" I looked helplessly at Andy and he smiled slightly at me.

"Put the weapon down!" Andy bellowed and I flinched involuntarily. He looked hurt but brushed it off. Jay kept his gaze on me and went to pull the trigger. He didn't get to though. Andy had tackled him to the ground. Now they are fighting.

Andy's black gun was thrown someplace and they are fighting over Jay's. I ran around them in search for the gun. It was hard to see considering it was late at night and the gun was black. I found it next to a tree and I picked it up. I held it up and took a couple steps closer to the two men fighting on the ground. They were nearing the edge of the cliff. "Stop!" I screamed.

They both froze in surprise. Andy hopped off of him and made his way over to my side with a proud smile. He stood behind me and I kept my eyes on the man who almost killed me moments ago. This is real. This is ridiculous.

Jay scrambled to his feet with a look of panic. "Reese, you don't want to shoot me. I raised you. I worked to make sure that you could go to school." He pleaded pathetically. I took another step forward and he jumped back a bit. He was less than an inch from the edge. "I love you." His words made something inside me snap.

"You don't love me. You never have." I said emotionlessly. Then I pulled the trigger. His lips parted and he stared blankly at me. His hands went to his stomach and he stumbled backwards with a look of shock.

"Y-you shot m-me," he coughed out. Then he disappeared. He fell off the cliff, into the water and crashing waves.

"Karma's a bitch." I muttered and then a single tear ran down my face. The realization of what I'd just done had hit me. I killed my step dad.

Andy put an arm around my shoulder and held me to his chest. "It's okay, You did good. It's all over now." He told me and walked me back to his car as he took me to the police station.

I walked in and went through everything. The questions and let them take care of my head. After that I saw three of the most amazing people ever enter the station. Graham, followed by Cameron and Adrienne. They all ran up to me wrapping me into a giant hug. Graham peppered kisses all over my face before landing on my lips.

"How'd you...know I was...here?" I asked between kisses. Graham just hugged me to him.

Adrienne laughed, "Andy called us. Told us what happened." She said and I nodded hugging Graham back as he breathed in my scent.

"Don't ever scare me like that again. I love you too much to have you get hurt." Graham mumbled against my shoulder.

"I love you too," I kissed his lips and he responded instantly. "I'm okay Graham I promise."

He looks at me like I'm crazy. "You're not okay. You will be though. I'll be here for you forever and I won't let anything happen to you again." He vowed.

"I'm glad you're okay." Cam says pulling me into a hug. I feel a tap on my shoulder and I turn to see Andy.

"You saved my life." He says and I smile.

"You saved mine too." I replied and thanked him.

"You are a very strong girl." He compliments and I smiled even wider before heading out with my friends.

I went to stay at Graham's house because Andy didn't want me staying at my own. Graham was more than happy to take me in. This time we both ended up sleeping in his bed and I was actually content and happy. This boy. I guess this is the end of my abuse. It's over, and I've never been happier.

EPILOGUE

I step into the living room of my house and plop down on the couch. "You're home pretty late." Graham says as I lay my head in his lap and he runs his fingers through my hair.

"I'm doing another movie." I huff out and he smiles at me.

"What it called?" He asked tilting his head which was super cute.

"You know that book, Run For Your Death?" I questioned and he nodded. "Well they are making it into a movie and I get to do the monster makeup. Now I just have to come up with a design tomorrow and get started on the costume." I explained to him sitting up so I could go and get some water.

"That's awesome," he says with one of his amazing smiles. I stop right outside of the kitchen.

"This is a big deal and trust me, it'll bring in a lot of money." I told him and he just smirked as I stepped into the kitchen.

Brianna with her big belly and her boyfriend, Nick were sat at the island in the kitchen. Nick had gotten Brianna pregnant. No, I know what you're wondering and they are not married. Although they act like a married couple. Brianna and I had became close friends over time. I got to know Nick a little better and he was actually a very nice guy.

Brianna squealed and gave me a side hug because her belly was too big to hug me normally. She was due on August thirteenth which was a little less than a month away. "You forgot about us didn't you?" Nick asked mockingly.

I smiled sheepishly and Brianna scoffed. "What a good friend you are." I knew she was kidding and soon after she shrugged. "Not that it matters. The others haven't shown up yet either."

I laughed and felt arms around my waist. I looked up into the eyes of Graham. He smiled down at me and the door bell rang. I walked to the door and opened it to see Cameron and his boyfriend at the door.

Although Mike and Cameron broken up, Cameron found a guy that was a year older than him when he went to collage. Now that they are out, they both have well paying jobs and a very heathy relationship. His name is Joni. He is very polite and he treated Cameron good.

Mike on the other hand, is single. He lives in New York now so I barely see him but he still visits sometimes. Cam and him are just friends now. They went to different collages and Mike never liked long distance relationships. He thought that they should try and see what it was like to be apart and Cam agreed. They found out that they were better as friends so that's the way they stayed. Then Cam found Joni.

They both hugged me apologizing for being late. Then I saw a car pull up in the front yard. Of course she parked in the yard. Adrienne hopped out of the car and ran up the steps almost jumping in my arms. Adrienne worked as a designer at a successful fashion firm. I don't quite remember what it's called. She has helped me with some of my designs and even made my dresses for special events or nice dinners. Unfortunately, she has been away in Hong Kong for the last month.

"Okay where's the food?" Was the first thing she said. I laughed as we walked toward the dinning room. Graham had already set the table and had all the food ready. Oh, how I love this man.

Adrienne sat down and very impatiently waited to eat. "Can we eat yet?" She whined.

I laughed at her and shook my head no. "We still need one more," I said and then the door bell rang again. I ran to the door and opened it to see a very laid back looking Andy.

"Come on! You take too long!" I yanked him into the dining room and forced him to take a seat. "Okay Adrienne now you can eat." She immediately dug into the macaroni and cheese.

"So what's new?" Cameron asked looking around the table. I smiled secretively and he narrowed his eyes at me.

Brianna spoke up before anyone else. "I'm due next month, but Nick won't let me watch the video to find out if it's a girl or a boy."

"I want it to be a surprise." He whined and she shook her head.

"If we have a boy after all the girl stuff we got I'm going to kill you." She glared whole heartedly at him. He gulped and nodded.

Andy cleared his throat. "I'm sherif now," he admits with a shrug. Andy had sort of became a father figure for me. He was the closest thing I had and was a great role-model. He even did me the favor of getting Graham on the force. Even though Andy's his boss Graham still loves him all the same. I think he noticed how much of a parental figure Andy is to me. Even though he's only about ten years older than me.

"Now not only is he my boss, but he's my bosses boss!" Graham exclaims.

"That's great, Andy." I laugh and he smiles at me.

"My turn!" Cameron says. "Me and Joni are going to the Bahamas. I need a vacation, but don't worry we'll be back before the baby is born." He says aloud then looks at Brianna.

Adrienne took this as her chance to talk. "Nothing new with me. I went on three dates and they all left within the first half an hour." She says shrugging. "Oh, I'm back for a long time! Until they send me away again. That won't be for a while though." She says with jazz hands. Oh wow.

I laugh at my best friend. I'm glad she's back. Also, you maybe be wondering what I do for a living. I'm a special effects makeup artist. I design the costumes and do the makeup you see in movies and television shows. The thing is that I love what I do. Now, I would tell my friends about the movie I'm working on but I've got something more important.

"So when's the date? I need to know so I can take off work or whatever." Adrienne asked and my eyes almost bulge out.

"We haven't planned it yet and no one else knows!" I snap at her and she mouths an apology. Everyone gives us weird glances, except Graham who had a knowing look.

"I thought we agreed to tell them as a group?" Graham's says with an eyebrow raised. I smiled sheepishly and he just smiles back, kissing me.

"What is going on?" An impatient Brianna shouts out. Graham's hand takes mine under the table and he lifts it up so people can see. I'm surprised no one noticed. I mean I never wear rings.

There are a bunch of gasps and a loud squeal. Brianna starts to cry. "My baby brother is growing up!" She says, using her hand to fan her eyes.

"I'm older than you," Graham says confused. She shh's him and he just laughs.

"I can't believe you're engaged!" Cameron says examining the ring. It was extremely beautiful. I loved it, and I loved it's meaning.

"It's about time!" Joni yells and we all laugh. All of my friends that are here congratulate me. Andy hugs me and I notice the tear that slid down his face. He really is amazing. He's like a real father. One of which I've never had. So I'm thankful.

As for Jay and that situation, he's dead and I killed him. That still haunts me. I couldn't believe I killed someone. Graham told me it had to be done. It just didn't feel right. Graham stood by me all the way though. Now we're getting married.

"I want you to help me with the wedding." I told Adrienne and she smiled hugging me tight.

"Of course I'll help," was her response.

"I also want you to be one of my maids of honor." I said and then that's when she squealed and crushed my bones with her arms.

I'm ecstatic. I have friends who I consider family and they love me. I have a job that I enjoy and I'm marrying the man of my dreams, who I love very much. I'm living the life!

"I got you something," Adrienne smirked as she handed me a bag. I expected boots or a cute dress but no. I put my hand down in the bag and pulled out some black and red laced lingerie. It was sexy, I'll admit.

Graham saw it and he smirked at me. Walking over and putting his arms around my waist. "Thanks," I say awkwardly to Adrienne who smirks even wider.

"Yeah, thanks Adrienne. That will be of use tonight." Graham adds, his voice sounding husky as he kisses my neck. My face feels like it's on fire and I already know my cheeks are red. Adrienne snickers and walks off.

Soon, it's just me and Graham in the house. I smile at himI'm adoration as we lay on the couch. I'm snuggle up to him and he is kissing my head and cheeks. His dad had dropped by yesterday.

He had gotten ten years in prison. He was just released and he didn't have to serve his ten years. When he saw his pregnant daughter I'm sure you could imagine his face. He looked like a fire truck.

Everything was okay now. Everyone was okay. My dad never came back but I kept in touch with my Aunt P. She met Graham and took a liking to him. I don't know how you couldn't like Graham. As for Holly, she's in rehab. Last time I saw her she was leaving a bar with a man twice her age. I feel bad for he but at least she's getting help. Maybe she'll clean herself up and do good.

As I lay on the couch with my fiancé I felt a certain joy bubble over. I snuggled into his side. "Pick a date," I said randomly.

Graham looked as if he was thinking for a minute besides he answered. "November twentieth." I smiled and kissed his soft lips.

"We're getting married on November twentieth." I said aloud and he smiled down at me. My life is great!